THE ALIEN'S REVELATION

GRACE KENSINGTON

1

———

Jonah could see the look of confusion and concern in Linnea's eyes but didn't know what to tell her. Asking her to come here had been a tremendous risk for her. The escape from the facility was still incredibly fresh in all their minds, even though time had passed, and they had all come to settle into the protection and comfort of Nana's house. She was putting herself in danger by agreeing to come back here without knowing what she might face. There was no way to know if Ryan was still watching the perimeter of the school or even still had members of his army patrolling the buildings to watch for any of the group to return so that he could get his hands on them again. I hadn't seen any of them or noticed any signs that they might still be watching, still waiting, still ready to try to take control again.

As I crept through the grounds and made my way back into the school I had been as vigilant as I possibly could, watching out of the corners of my eyes and trying to remain as aware of the feelings within my body. Something that I had learned in the time since I was working in the old version of this school was to listen to my body and trust what it told me. I was within my body but at the same time, it was as though my body was its own entity. It could tell me far more about what was happening in a situation than I could be aware of in an instant. I trusted myself and allowed myself to tune in to the shivers down my spine, the stinging of my skin, or the sense of heaviness that settled over my head when I was walking into a situation that could be dangerous. It had taken me so long to really learn that. I had been through so much, suffered so much, witnessed so much.

But in the moments when I let myself breathe, I was thankful for all of it, because it had taught me the invaluable lesson that I knew had saved my life countless times before. It was something that took only a second. There was a moment, a brief moment, when what I felt could prepare me for what may lay a step ahead. If I took that moment, I could be ready. If I didn't, I may not live to see what may be in the step beyond that.

I could remember a time, distantly it felt like, when I had to pause and connected myself inward in order to evaluate what I was feeling and what might be happening around me. The thought of being able to do that seemed like a luxury now. I no longer had it. Now I was in a constant state of vigilance, my senses heightened, my mind focused, and my muscles tense. I had to be if I wanted to get through this alive.

I'd had that same vigilance from the moment I arrived back on the campus and since then I hadn't noticed any feelings that told me there was any imminent danger. There was the expected swirl of discomfort through my belly and tightness of bitter nostalgia in my chest. I knew that would be there. It always would be. Walking through these grounds felt as if my feet were trying to find the footsteps I had left so long before and entering buildings that were foreign and familiar, new and old, mine and beyond my grasp. There were layers there. Layers of time. Layers of experience. Layers of existence.

But I hadn't felt the eyes of the Valdicians on me. I hadn't heard the timed breaths of the hybrids. I hadn't seen the people walking through the campus, looking as though they were trying to blend in with the world around them but standing out even more because of it. Even as I thought that, I wondered what other people thought when they saw them. Every day people swarmed the campus grounds and the buildings rising out of them. Students, teachers, and workers of all kinds roamed around oblivious to all that was happening just beneath their feet or even right in front of their eyes. Jonah knew these people saw the hybrids. They may even see the Valdicians. Ryan didn't hesitate to take the most seamlessly crafted of his army and send them out among the throng so they could watch everything that was happening and bring back the details of everything they saw and heard.

Jonah wondered if the people who belonged on the campus noticed them. Many of the hybrids were created so delicately that their looks barely differentiated them from other species that already existed among the humans on the campus. Some even looked nearly entirely human themselves. But there were differences. Many of them walked in a stilted, controlled way that came from never having the opportunity to develop normally but rather being forced into growth and learning nearly from the moment of birth. Once the hybrid babies were born, they were brought to the nursery where they were monitored and processed rather than cared for and nurtured. New skills such as walking and talking weren't seen as milestones, but programming stages. Some responded more smoothly than others and Jonah had seen those who had been freed gradually losing these behaviors and compulsions.

Those who were still in Ryan's grasp had been further indoctrinated and Jonah knew that most if not all of them would have mannerisms that would totally separate them from anyone around them. But would the people around them actually notice? Something else Jonah had learned was that people, especially when they were in large groups, tended to be very easy to distract and convince. People in a group didn't want to be different. They didn't want to be the ones whose thoughts didn't fall in line with those of everyone around them. They didn't want to be the ones who brought attention to something others didn't notice or hadn't seemed to bother anyone else. When people were alone they were sometimes more likely to notice strange things or to question what they were seeing, but simply guiding them toward noticing what others around them were seeing or thought could put them right back into control.

This was a benefit in many ways. Trusting and being willing to follow could mean protection and less resistance. But it could also be extremely dangerous. When people put so much of their reliance and trust in the people around them, and stopped putting their trust in themselves, they were no longer able to guard themselves. Their fear of being separated from the group kept them from noticing what could put them all at risk.

Jonah knew that was what was happening with the hybrids that were sent out amongst the students and teachers of the University campus. They could be a serious threat, a danger that none of those who came to the University each day to study or to work would understand, and they might not even be prepared to respond. Did any of them notice the strangers moving among them? If they did, how did they feel when they were near them? What did they think when they saw them? Would they react if needed?

Learning that Ryan had begun to send his hybrids out on the campus, both from the main facility itself and the outposts he had created, had made it more intimidating to choose this spot for where he would meet with Linnea, but also made it more urgent. He knew the danger he could be facing by coming back here again. Before, the hybrids moved only in a formation and only when Ryan was in control, restricting their movements to battles and training, and primarily at night. Then there was a shift. Jonah didn't know the exact moment when the change happened. He only knew that Ryan had noticed him there and within hours he saw a hybrid step out of the building and into the flow of people walking by. The man, a blend that Jonah would assume was primarily human and Mikana, had carried nothing and looked nowhere but ahead. He walked with determination and direction, but when Jonah fell into step several feet behind him, following his path, he found that he walked to one end of the campus, turned, walked across the other direction, and then turned again and headed back toward the building where he began. He didn't enter any of the buildings, he didn't interact with anyone. By the next day, their numbers had grown.

He knew Ryan was looking for them. He wanted to reclaim his creations and ensure that the pregnant women were contained before they gave birth, so all the babies would know was his facility. But he wanted Jonah, Aubrey, and Ilya more.

That was what brought Jonah here now. That was why

he had asked Linnea to do something so dangerous. He didn't want her to be in harm's way. He wanted to protect her just as much as he wanted to protect all the others and find a way to free those who were still held in Ryan's grasp. But he needed her help. To accomplish what he needed to, he had to have someone with knowledge not only of Ryan's operations, but also of what was happening with the rest of the crew. The truth was, what Jonah was doing may have been an even greater risk.

He had been moving this way for so long, and yet this was one of the very few times when he ever felt any sense of being nervous. Traveling was never the term that he felt like using to describe his movements. That didn't seem to give the right impression, the right definition to how he was able to shift and explore, to exist in first one moment and reality and then in another, but also in both. It had been after he had come back here three times that he went to Linnea and asked for her help. He told her everything, explaining the critical importance of what he needed to do. It was the first time that he had explained it to anyone who wasn't sharing his timeline and he worried about how she was going to react. She could have laughed at him. She could have been enraged that he would have tried to manipulate or confuse her.

Instead, she believed him.

Jonah could only imagine that after an entire lifetime that was built around someone trying to destroy the Universe and all that was in it, Linnea was eager to believe in someone who was trying to save it.

But this was the first time that he had asked her to come back here and it was the first time that he wouldn't leave immediately after their meeting. He was preparing for what could be the most dangerous mission that he had ever taken, and he didn't know what was going to happen. Before now each time that Jonah had moved from time to time or stream to stream it had been for brief visits or he knew that he was going to be far from the rest of the group. This wasn't the case now. His realities were about to crash into one another and if he wasn't careful with how he timed each movement he could cause irreparable damage. He didn't really know what would happen if they saw him. He didn't know what would happen if he saw himself.

He only knew that he couldn't let it happen. He had to bide his time and make sure that he was there at the exact moment when he left. If he wasn't, the world around him and all that they had known could dissolve away.

2

George slept only a short time before the questions burning in the back of his mind woke him up. He turned the lamp back on and picked up the dish he had put on the table beside him. He stared at the leaf, examining the color and the veins, remembering the last time that he had seen something like this. It had surprised him then, but he hadn't said anything about it. There was too much else going on for him to mention the type of leaf that was chosen to be in a bracelet. While it had been intriguing to him then, it had seemed inconsequential and he hadn't wanted to distract anyone or take up any of the time and energy that they needed to be devoting to what was really happening in order to explore his scientific curiosity.

Now it seemed that it could possibly mean so much more. There was no way he could have known it then, but now that he was seeing the leaf in his hand, things seemed to be gradually piecing together, though there were still huge gaps that would need to be filled. For now, he would start with the leaf.

Climbing out of the bed, he dressed and walked out of the room. He intended to go back to the infirmary to examine the man further, though he didn't know for sure what he was hoping he would find or what it might tell him. On his way, however, he heard a voice in one of the smaller rooms. His steps slowed, and he listened again, trying to discern from which room the voice was coming. It was a woman's voice, the tone low and soft as she seemed to be trying to quiet someone. It sounded familiar and he knew that it was Ivy. He followed the sound until it brought him into the lounge and he hesitated, watching her as she paced a short path back and forth in front of a window. The shields were down, preventing her from being able to look out, but he could only imagine that she was envisioning what was beyond.

"Ivy?" he finally said.

She turned and looked at him. George's eyes lowered to the bundle in his arms and he smiled. He would never have imagined Ivy as a mother. His young assistant was vibrant and energetic, driven and focused, but all that energy and drive went into her work. She had never seemed interested in anything beyond a life that was devoted fully to science and any time she discussed what her future may hold for her, it was only her hopes of having her own laboratory or making the discoveries that would change the world. Never had she mentioned she might one day like to find someone to settle down with or to have a child. She had never expressed any interest in having a life that would bring her thoughts or energies even the smallest distance from the problems and questions that plagued her, but that she truly believed she would be able to solve with discoveries and connections they constantly sought. It was like the world, life, all of existence was a puzzle and she was forever looking for the pieces that were going to bring it together. That was her contribution. That was what she was going to give to the world.

Now that had changed. Though the passion for science was still obvious in her, when she went to Uoria she made what was likely the most valuable and meaningful of all the discoveries she had ever made. And that was herself. She found out who she really was when she got onto the planet and had to make the decision of whether she would combine forces with George and the rest of the women in the Denynso compound to help the men release those later discovered to be the Nyx 23 crew. She learned even more when she agreed to travel across the planet and then found Maxim. In Maxim, she uncovered realities about herself and about the life she had never known and that she would never have found if she had stayed in the laboratories on Earth. Now she cradled their child in her arms, a child who was more precious and more impactful than they could have ever imagined. This child, who had been given such a meaningful and beautiful name by her grandfather, was a brand-new species, a brand-new race, the ruler of a planet that had been given up as ravaged and worthless but could now be cleansed and redeemed from its brutal past.

"She was having trouble sleeping," Ivy explained.

She looked so natural holding Dove in her arms, gazing down into her tiny face. Her daughter was less than a day old and had already made so much of a difference. She had already changed everything.

"Is she alright now?" George asked, stepping further into the room.

Ivy nodded.

"She's fine."

"Maybe she's just eager to see her planet," George said with a smile.

Ivy looked as though she was trying to smile as well, but there was worry in her eyes that even her tremendous joy and pride couldn't cover.

"Do you really think that she is going to be safe?" she asked.

"I really do. I think her birth is a turning point. This planet doesn't represent what it used to."

"That's the thing. Everyone is saying Penthos belongs to her now and that she is the ruler of it. But Ryan is still absolutely in control. The planet is crawling with his hybrids. We don't even know how many are here. And you know that he's watching. Somehow, he knows everything that's happening. He has slaughtered countless people and has made absolutely no hesitation in stating it is his intention to take over the galaxy first and the entirety of the Universe next. He has no problem destroying entire species and obliterating what is in his way. The birth of one little baby girl isn't going to change that, even if it did happen on a previously unclaimed planet."

"But that's it, Ivy. It was previously unclaimed. It belonged to no one and to nothing. Do you think it was an accident that Ryan chose to come back to this planet to continue the efforts that his ancestors began? Penthos was taken over long ago to be used for the prison colony by the Valdicians. We know that. But they never claimed it for themselves. They never said that it belonged to them. Then when it was supposedly liberated by the military, Earth didn't claim it, either. Then Ryan chose to return here to work on his experiments and train them for battle. This ground is to be used for war, but it belonged to no one. Until now."

"I don't understand."

"The Universe is bigger and more complex than any of us can imagine. We looked at it in such a closed, miniscule way when we were on Earth in that laboratory. We thought that we knew about the planets and even the rims of wild space. But we were so incredibly wrong. We've learned there is so much more. Think about Jem. Think about how he disappeared and then came back. He traveled. He went somewhere that we don't know. That means that there's far more that is yet to be understood. Thinking about someone who is trying to drag all of that under his own control is unfathomable. So, we break things down. We think of each of the species. We think of the threats he has made to Uoria. But we still planned for war somewhere technically neutral. Though he had his grips on it first and was able to establish troops on it, it is still not his. It doesn't belong to him. But it does belong to her. We are fighting for the safety and preservation of all existence and we aren't fighting on unclaimed ground anymore. Ryan and every one of his hybrids is an invader They are on ground that belongs to Dove and to the future that she is going to make."

"He'll want her," Ivy said.

"Of course, he will," George told her. "But he can't have her. We will defend her just as we are defending Maxim and Kyven. He can't have them, and he can't destroy them. We'll take him down first."

"How? We're so fractured. We're so spread out. There so many still on Uoria and even more on Earth. We don't know what they're doing or why. How are we possibly going to come together to fix this?"

"Because we maybe already have."

Ivy's expression became confused and she shook her head slightly.

"What do you mean?"

"I found something on the body that Rilex and Severine brought up from the tunnels. It looked so familiar and then it struck me. I'm not completely sure what it means, but it's enough to tell me that we are closer than we thought."

"What was it?"

George withdrew the dish from his pocket and offered it to Ivy. She balanced the baby in one arm and took the dish, bringing it closer so that she could look at it in the light that she had kept dim as to not disturb her sleeping child.

"Do you recognize it?" George asked.

Ivy narrowed her eyes and seemed to lean a little closer.

"I'm not sure," she said. "I feel like it looks familiar, but I can't put my finger on it."

"Can you come to the infirmary with me?"

Ivy nodded and handed the dish with the leaf back to George.

"Let me bring her back into the pod with Maxim so she can sleep. I'll meet you there."

George nodded. and they went separate directions down the hallway. He headed back toward the infirmary where the body was still spread out across the table. He placed the dish on another of the tables and walked back to the body, turning the vibrant overhead light on and pulling it down closer to the body so that he could focus his attention on each small section of the bones. The tips of his fingers were running along the bones, feeling each detail and his mind chronicling feelings of past injuries that might have affected the man.

"Anything interesting?"

George looked over his shoulder and saw Ivy coming into the infirmary. She had changed out of the nightgown she had been wearing and her thick blond hair was coiled up on the top of her head much as she would often wear it in the lab on Earth. She looked like she was trying to put herself back in her element, to bring herself back into the role that was so familiar to her, almost as if she needed to completely separate herself from the changes that had come over her since she arrived on Uoria so she could focus again, so she could step back into being his assistant.

"This man went through a lot," George said. "He didn't have an easy life."

"There are injuries?"

"More than I can count. They are layered on top of each other so much that it seems he found himself in pretty brutal circumstances over the course of many years. He must have seen some horrible things."

"But why? Was he a soldier?"

"The clothing he's wearing doesn't look a uniform. At least, what's left of it doesn't look like it was a uniform. Besides, there don't appear to be any of the types of injuries that are consistent with warfare, except very specific circumstances of hand-to-hand combat. This looks more like injuries from accidents like falls. And torture."

"Torture?" Ivy asked, her voice low.

George nodded.

"It looks like he went through incredible violence."

"Is that why he ended up down in the tunnels? He was killed and thrown down there?"

"I don't think so. According to Rilex and Severine, he wasn't just lying there. He didn't look like he had been thrown or anything. He was on his stomach clutching a book. That doesn't seem like something a person would be doing if they had been killed and tossed down into tunnels to be forgotten."

"Then why was he down there?"

"I'm still not sure. I haven't been able to find a specific cause of death. But I found that leaf clinging to him and it reminded me of something."

"What?"

"Do you remember when we were first researching the Denynso and we read that account about the war that they were involved in thousands of years ago?"

"The war that they were called in to be a part of just a few years after the clan had divided?"

"Yes."

"I thought we discredited that happening because it was only that one account and it contradicted itself. The timing of when it supposedly happened changes in the middle of the account and it mentions a planet that was never found."

"But what if it doesn't actually contradict itself?"

"But it doesn't make sense. There are two different timelines and it says that the planet exists inside a constellation."

"If there's one thing that we've learned since leaving Earth for Uoria it is that things aren't always what they seem. There are two timelines in the account, but what if both of them are accurate? You heard Rilex and Jem talking about how he was able to survive his disappearance because he ended traveling through a portal and into a different stream. What if that's what happened during that war? It happened in two different times and on two different planets because it actually happened in two different streams?"

"What does that have to do with a leaf that you found on the body?"

"Think about the papers that were with the account. One of them had sketches of the plants from the planet where the war originated. One looked exactly like that leaf."

"You think that this body is a person from a planet that

was supposed to have been destroyed in a war?" Ivy asked, sounding incredulous.

George shook his head.

"Not destroyed. Abandoned. Evacuated. Remember? It said that before the main fighting of the war that the inhabitants of the planet were gathered up and removed. An entire species was taken from the planet and put on another one to keep it protected during the war and after. There is no record of where that other planet was or whatever might have happened to the people who were put there. But there also isn't any indication that after the war the original planet didn't just continue on, empty."

"Penthos?" Ivy asked.

"No. Not Penthos. Nothing so close."

"Do you think that you know where that planet might be?"

"I don't, but I think that we might know a few people who could. The first time that I talked to Jem I noticed that he was wearing a bracelet. He said that Angela made it for him as a Christmas gift when they were still in the stream where he went after disappearing from Uoria, before he connected with Rilex and came back here. He said that she made it out of grasses and leaves from that planet." George walked over to the table and picked up the dish. "Some of those leaves looked exactly like this."

Ivy's eyes snapped up to George and widened.

"I think that we need to talk to Jem."

George nodded.

"And Rilex."

3

———

"What did you mean?"

Lucian turned sharply as if startled by the sound of Mhavrych's voice.

"Excuse me?"

Mhavrych took a few more steps toward the Eteri, his eyes locked on the pools of blue in the other man's face. He had left the frozen exile under the guise of allowing Casimir and Aegeus time to reconnect, but he had known the moment that he walked away from them that there was something else that he needed to be doing. The face of the woman who called herself Kendra, the woman who claimed to be his wife, hadn't been far from his mind, but he knew that finding out who she was and what she meant wasn't going to be as simple as just asking her. There was a reason that she was baiting him, a reason that she was teasing him and playing with him in that way rather than just approaching him. It had to do with why she had the star stone and Mhavrych knew it went further than her. He couldn't imagine why he would have given her the stone rather than keeping it to protect it or bringing it home to his parents. Even more, he couldn't understand how it was possible that he could forget not only meeting this woman but marrying her. He needed to unravel what was happening and that meant going to the person who was both closest to her and that knew more than he should. Lucian.

"When we were in the meeting you said that you knew so much because the rocks had a way of talking to you. What did you mean by that?"

Lucian looked at him with an expression that was difficult to discern. In a way, it seemed confused, but there was also happiness there, amusement that Mhavrych was coming to him.

"I meant exactly what I said," Lucian said. "The rocks have a way of talking to you, if you are willing to listen."

"What does that mean?"

"Why are you asking?"

"You know things you shouldn't," Mhavrych said. "And I believe that you know more than you're saying. You know why that woman Kendra came here with you."

"She came to help, just like the rest of the Eteri."

Mhavrych shook his head.

"No. The rest that came are warriors. She isn't a warrior. She came here for me, and you know why. Tell me."

"I believe that she has something of yours that she wanted to return to you."

The Eteri man didn't specifically say he knew that she had a star stone, and for the first time Mhavrych didn't feel as though he were lying to him or trying to avoid saying something. It was possible Lucian really didn't know what it was that Kendra was carrying or the significance it held.

"I don't know her," Mhavrych said, hoping that might encourage the man to give him more details about why she seemed to know him and how she got the stone. "I have never met her."

"That's not what she seems to think."

"How did you know about Fayat? How did you know about his link with the Order? That's something no one is supposed to know."

"I already told you. The rocks told me."

Mhavrych felt frustration and anger building inside of him.

"Stop speaking in riddles and just tell me what I want to know. No one is supposed to know that but the Order and those who entrusted them. No one is supposed to know about the link between the Valdicians and the Denynso."

"But they already know," Lucian said. "You've already met the descendant of Aida and Fayat, the one who still carries the Valdician blood. He's strong enough that he can move things with his mind but has the skills of the warriors."

"They know that a child was born to them and that the child was raised among the Denynso, going on to continue the bloodline. But the Order ended the alliance with the Denynso when they sent Aida and Fayat to the distant planet. The breaking of that link was meant to protect them."

"But it didn't," Lucian said.

"What do you mean?"

"Think of all that's happened since then. Think of all the danger that has come to Uoria and those who live here since that one decision was made. There has been division and war. Bloodshed. Disappearances. You can't truly believe that those are unrelated."

"Lucian, I need you to tell me everything that you know."

"Why?"

"I was sent here to find something invaluable, something

that could destroy or defend the entire Universe. But it has been held in absolute secrecy since long before anyone on this planet lived, or generations before them. If you know that secret, then that means others may as well, and what I need to do is even more urgent than before."

"What I said in that meeting is what I know," Lucian said. "I don't know what happened before Fayat and Aida and I don't know what happened after. What I do know is that seems to be the time when the alliances on Uoria started to dissolve and things were set into motion that are now coming to a head."

Mhavrych nodded.

"Can you show me the rocks?" he asked. "The rocks that told you this. Can you show them to me?"

Lucian nodded.

"I could, but that would mean going back to the Eteri kingdom. We've only just gotten here to help Creia."

"I understand that," he said. "But Creia wants the same thing that I do. To end the danger and protect the planet and the Universe. He is fighting against Ryan. My responsibilities, my fight, started long before him. I know that he called for your help. The alliance of his kind with yours is long-running, but I need you to trust that the alliance of my kind with the Denynso goes back just as far, if not farther. I need to understand what you know, and I need to understand what link I have to Kendra. It could be instrumental in finally bringing this to a close."

"We'll talk to Creia," Lucian said. "I'll tell him that I can put another of my warriors in command and they are authorized to act whenever and however necessary. I'll bring you to the kingdom and show you the rocks and return as soon as I can."

"Thank you."

. . .

LATER THAT EVENING Mhavrych and Lucian walked out of the room where they had met with Creia. The Denynso king followed, his face drawn.

"Thank you for your understanding, Creia."

"Are you sure that you know what you're doing?"

Mhavrych nodded.

"The Valdicians are at the core of all of this. They are the source of the destruction. What's happening now isn't new. They've taken their time and they've seen challenges and opposition, but their plans are coming due now. Everything that's been happening -- it's not accidental. It's not coincidental. This is all connected and unless we address every thread, we'll never prevail. The Universe is going to fall to them."

"Go," Creia said. "Do what needs to be done. Trust that I will do my part here."

"We'll come back together soon," Mhavrych promised. "Aegeus and Casimir will return soon and we will meet on the battlefield on Penthos."

Creia gave a single nod and Mhavrych and Lucian rushed away from the building, into the growing darkness. For a moment Mhavrych considered guiding the Eteri toward the tunnels, but he hesitated. He had been using them too much. He had been relying on the ancient form of traveling too heavily and had become careless. Though he wanted to believe that he could trust Lucian, if even just so that he could follow him and get the information that he needed, Mhavrych knew that he needed to be cautious. He needed to protect himself and the rest by avoiding the tunnels and the portals as much as possible.

As they had discussed, Lucian used a thick strap to wrap

around his own waist and then around Mhavrych's, tying the two men together. He then took hold of Mhavrych with one arm around his chest and rose up into the sky, beginning to fly toward the Eteri kingdom. It would take far longer than moving through the portals, and it would leave Lucian exhausted, but it would keep the planet more secure.

MHAVRYCH'S WAIST stung from the strap biting into him and his muscles ached from trying to hold himself up while they flew by the time that they finally made it to the kingdom. He couldn't wait to be free of the Eteri man and to be able to move on his own. He hated the feeling of being helpless and not being able to control where he was going or what he was doing. When the ground was beneath his own feet again, he removed the strap and took several long strides away from Lucian so that he could feel the emptiness around him.

"Where do we go now?" he asked.

"I need some time to refresh myself," Lucian said. "You are welcome to come to my home with me."

"No. I'll stay here," Mhavrych said. "Meet me back here when you're ready."

"I will."

Mhavrych tried not to feel frustrated or angry toward the man for not continuing on with their mission immediately, reminding himself that Lucian had flown the entire way across the planet and would need a chance to rest and rejuvenate himself. Mhavrych walked around the clearing where Lucian had left him, looking at the lush plants that surrounded it and feeling the cool breeze. The air was softer here than it was in the Mikana kingdom and Mhavrych filled his lungs with it, letting it release some of the tension inside of him. He followed the sound of water to the edge of a tiny creek and knelt down to fill his palm with the crystal water. Bringing it to his lips, he marveled in its cool sweetness, feeling almost instantly refreshed and re-energized by it.

"Why are you here?"

Mhavrych saw the reflection and heard the voice before he saw the person standing in front of him. Her image shimmered in the water and he could see tiny flecks of pink fluttering to the surface of the creek as it swept by. He lifted his eyes to her as he straightened, not wanting to move too quickly in case she decided to run from him again.

"What are you doing here?" he asked. "You were in the Mikana kingdom."

"So were you."

"But why did you come back?"

"Why are you here?"

"Lucian brought me," Mhavrych responded. "I need him to show me something that he knows."

"But you already know," Kendra said. "You already know everything that you need to."

Mhavrych shook his head.

"No," he said. "I don't."

"Yes, you do. You know who you are. Trust yourself. Because everyone else trusts you."

"I don't understand," Mhavrych said. "Who are you? Why do you say that you're my wife? How do you have that star stone?"

"Because I am your wife," she said matter-of-factly. "And you gave me this stone."

"But I don't even remember meeting you."

"You will."

"But I'm here now. You can give me the stone."

Kendra shook her head.

"No," she said. "Not yet. It's not time yet. You said that you would come for it. You haven't come for it."

"What do you mean?"

Mhavrych could hear footsteps coming toward him and Kendra started to back away from the creek, her hand coming up to grip the starstone around her neck again.

"Come find me," she said softly. "Follow me."

Before Mhavrych could ask her what she meant or take a step to follow her, Lucian emerged back into the clearing and she disappeared back into the thick forest behind her.

"Are you ready?" Lucian asked.

MHAVRYCH STALKED ANGRILY into the palace, not pausing when he saw the startled look on his mother's face.

"You said that the portals were sealed. You told me that there was no way to go back."

"Mhavrych, what are you talking about?" Galadriel asked.

"You told me that there was no way to control movement through the streams. That there were only the portals that have always existed, and they were the only way to travel."

Galadriel and Vyker exchanged glances. He could see the unsure, unsteady expression on his mother's face, the expression that came when she questioned how much she knew about her husband's kind and planet, and how much she didn't. She had lived the majority of her life on Earth in a time countless years ahead of the time she lived in now. Though she had worked hard to learn the ways and the history of the man who she devoted her life to and the new existence that she had chosen, there was so much that was different here and she had discovered this world in a time of fire and upheaval, throwing herself into it well before she understood any of it. This left her often feeling as though she was at the mercy of her husband and had to rely on him completely to tell her what was happening and how to respond. Now was one of those moments and Mhavrych could see it. She knew something, but she didn't know what she should say.

"What's happened, Mhavrych?" Vyker asked.

Mhavrych looked at his father and took another step toward him.

"My entire life you've told me that the only way that we could travel through the streams was in the specific ways that the portals existed, and that there was no way to manipulate it. You told me there was no way to decide where to travel except to the set points of the portals and that you couldn't travel to the same moment more than once. You lied to me."

"We didn't lie."

"Yes, you did. None of that is true."

"We didn't lie, Mhavrych. We guarded you. It isn't safe to play in the streams. They can be dangerous and manipulating time can cause disaster that you weren't prepared to face."

"But you thought I was prepared to be Protector. You thought I was prepared to defend the entire existence of the Universe."

"I didn't know the streams could be used that way until I was already an adult," Vyker said. "When I was younger and even when I was searching for the stones, I didn't know. I trusted what Rilex told me."

"When I met him, he told me the same," Galadriel said. "He said that we couldn't move through time in the traditional way but could only use portals to bring us to specific points."

"But you knew that wasn't true."

"What do you mean?" Vyker asked.

"You traveled through the streams and were always able to determine when you returned here. You came back at the moment that you wanted to. Mother, you traveled from here to Earth and back several times. Never did you have to worry that you were going to miss years and never be able to recover them. So obviously you were manipulating the portals so that you could travel to the moment you wanted to."

"I didn't know what I was doing," Galadriel said. "I traveled however and wherever they were going to bring me. I didn't have any control."

"But he did," Mhavrych said, looking at his father. "You had control and you knew that you did."

"Not until I was older, Mhavrych. I didn't realize what I was doing then. And when I did, it was because I was being faced with the reality of just how dangerous it could be. You have an incredibly important responsibility."

"One that I can't fulfill if you don't give me all of the information and skills that I need. You don't know what's been happening."

"I know more than you think you do. I was there. I've seen the things that you are just learning about."

"And you couldn't stop them. I have to," Mhavrych shouted, slamming his fist into his chest. "Too many people have died and there are so many more that could be decimated."

"That isn't your job," Vyker said intensely. "Your duty as Protector is to find the crest and bring it back here to be restored."

"I've found it," Mhavrych said.

"Then where is it?"

"It's secured on Uoria."

"It needs to be brought here," Vyker demanded. "The streams are at risk until you do."

"No," Mhavrych said, shaking his head. "There are more star stones that need to be found."

"How do you know that?"

"Because I've seen them. At least one of them. And even when I find it, that's not enough. I have been helping Casimir and Aegeus my entire life. I have known their fight since I was a child. But you never told me that it was my fight all along. You never told me where it all began."

"You didn't need to know."

"How can you say that? How can you expect me to protect something when I don't even know what I'm protecting? Do you know what they did to him? What he survived?"

Galadriel's eyes widened.

"Aegeus is alive?"

Mhavrych started to back away from them.

"I have to go," he said.

"Where are you going?" Vyker asked.

"Back."

4

───────

Ilya could still taste Mordecai's kiss and wanted another. She wanted to lean through the darkness of the closet again and press her lips to his, to forget all that was happening and pretend, if only for a moment, that they were somewhere safe. As she did, though, she heard a crashing sound that brought a gasp to her throat. Mordecai reached forward and pressed his hand across her mouth to quiet her.

"Shhhhh," he murmured in her ear. "Quiet. Stay still."

There was another crash and this time Ilya could tell that it was the sound of doors being kicked open.

"Where are you?" Ryan's voice called down the hallway in a sing-song tone that sent a shiver through her and turned her stomach. "Where are you, Ilya? Come out and talk to me." Another crash. "I just want to see you." Another crash. "I've been thinking, and I was wrong to keep you imprisoned in the facility." Another crash. "You were right." Another crash. "We should be a family."

The next kick was so loud that it seemed Ryan was nearly at the closet where they were hiding. Ilya could feel

Mordecai pulling on her, guiding her to her feet. He pointed up and she followed his gesture to a hatch in the ceiling.

"We can climb up there," he whispered.

"Come on, Ilya," Ryan's voice taunted. "I want to see you. I want to see our baby growing in your belly."

Another crash and Ilya shivered.

"I can't," she said. "I can't fit through the hatch. What are we going to do?"

The next crash made the door to the closet shake and she knew that Ryan was only feet away.

"We run," Mordecai said. "That's all we can do. We have to run. I'm going to open the door and you run as fast as you can. I'll hold him back and I'll follow you when I get a chance. Don't worry about me. Just run."

"Aubrey?" Jonah hissed into the inky darkness of the basement. "Aubrey, where are you?"

"Quiet," Aubrey scolded from somewhere close to him. "You don't want anybody to hear us. You need to hide."

"Where are you? We need to get out of here."

"We can't. We have to find out what the Valdicians are using the Izalux for. We can't just leave. We're this close."

"Ryan knows we're here," Jonah said. "We have to leave."

"No."

Jonah heard footsteps and thought that they were moving toward the door to the basement. He knew that she wanted to go back out into the factory, but he had to stop her. He couldn't let Ryan get to her. He started toward the door but felt his heart pound painfully as a dark figure stepped into his path. Jonah started to strike, but the figure stepped back and held up a hand.

"I don't mean you any harm," he said. "I need you to come with me."

"Come with you?" Jonah asked.

"Yes. Hurry."

"I can't. My wife could be hurt."

"Your wife will be in more danger if you don't come with me. I can't explain myself right now, but you need to come. You have to trust me that Aubrey will be safe."

"How am I supposed to trust that?" Jonah asked. "I don't even know who you are."

"My name is Frederick. I..." he hesitated. "I know Nana."

Jonah nodded, and Frederick let out a breath, returning the nod. He started toward the opposite side of the basement and Jonah fell into step behind him.

AUBREY HEARD a crash and started to run toward it. She could hear Ryan's voice and with every step closer she felt more anger toward him. Everything had happened around her so quickly, forcing her through it at a pace that was dizzying, barely allowing her a moment to breathe much less to think about how it was all affecting her. She had allowed herself to carry through by the intensity of her curiosity and how important it was to Jonah to understand what had happened before he climbed aboard the ship that brought him to Uoria so many years before. Now that she knew more, she was angry. Now that she had been given the opportunity to see more of the reality of Ryan and the disgusting unfolding of his plans, she could feel a fury burning within her that was unlike anything that she had ever experienced. It felt like her blood was boiling, searing through her veins and pushing her to run harder toward his voice.

She reached the hallway where she could hear his voice and held up a lightstick that she had tucked into her pocket.

"Ryan," she shouted. He stopped and whirled around to face her. His eyes widened when he saw her and then she noticed a grisly smile curl his lips. She dropped the lightstick, shoving it back into her pocket to block the light so that he couldn't see her as easily. "Come and get me."

She started running, her feet pounding on the floor as she followed her memory of the steps that she had taken back through the factory. She didn't know where she was going or even what she intended to do. All she could think about was running. His footsteps were getting louder, and Aubrey knew that he was getting closer. He called for the Valdicians and fear rushed through her, forcing her to go faster. As she turned a corner she felt the breath get knocked out of her by an arm grabbing her around the stomach from another hallway. She screamed, but a hand crashed down over her mouth. The arm pulled her back hard and she felt herself crush against a hard chest. A mouth came to her ear and she could feel hot breath on her skin as a voice whispered in her ear.

"Be quiet. I've got you. Just stay right here, stay quiet."

Aubrey nearly collapsed with relief as she realized that it was Jonah who held her. She rested back against him and squeezed her eyes closed, focusing on keeping her breath as even and quiet as she could. Ryan's footsteps got louder and then they were right outside the door. There was a brief moment of hesitation and the fear tightened in Aubrey's stomach again as she worried he might have either somehow detected that she and Jonah were standing there, or that she would make a noise and reveal them. Ryan continued, shouting for more of his Valdicians and for Aubrey. Occasionally he would scream out to Ilya and Aubrey worried more for the heavily pregnant woman.

"Come on," Jonah said. "We need to go. We need to get out of here."

"We can't leave the others."

"Aubrey, we have to leave. Now. The others will find their way."

The force in Jonah's voice caught Aubrey's attention and she knew that she couldn't fight him. She had already resisted his guidance and was nearly caught by Ryan. Nodding, she let Jonah step in front of her and look around to ensure that there was no one else around. Confirming that they were safe with a touch to her arm, he started out of their hiding place and Aubrey started after him. She felt breathless as she followed him through the factory and toward a section that she hadn't yet been in. She could hear movement throughout the building and knew that the Valdicians were coming after them. Not knowing where she was going and trying to navigate the halls in the near-darkness was unnerving and she felt herself getting so close to Jonah as they went that she nearly tripped over his feet.

"Where are we going?" she asked. "I thought that we were going down into the basement to meet with the others."

"We need to get out of the building. They'll find their way."

Aubrey squeezed closer to him and they continued through the hallways. Aubrey resisted the temptation to pull her lightstick out of her pocket. She wanted the illumination, but she didn't want to pull any more attention to them than they already were with the sound of their feet and their gasping breaths. Finally, she saw the outline of a window ahead. She knew that she had gone up and down several flights of steps when running from Ryan but had lost track of exactly where she was in the building, making her unsure of how high they actually were. She felt nervous as Jonah broke away pieces of plywood that had been put up over the window. Aubrey assumed this meant this was one of the windows that had been broken by some of the people who broke into the factory.

It felt strange thinking about people coming here thinking that it was a fun adventure, throwing rocks up at the building thinking that it was nothing but a prank. Even those who came back with harrowing tales of the factory being haunted usually told their tale with at least a hint of a smile on their lips as if even if they did believe that there was something there, the thrill was enough to justify what fear there might have been. Aubrey would never be able to look at the factory that way. She would never be able to see this place as anything less than horrifying.

The sound of the Valdicians was getting louder and Aubrey reached up to help him pull down the last of the wood planks. She glanced through the window and saw that while they weren't extremely high in the building, they were still further up than she felt comfortable with.

"Go on," Jonah said. "You need to get down."

"We're too high," Aubrey protested. "I can't jump."

"You have to," Jonah said. "There's nowhere else to go. You need to jump."

Aubrey knew that she had no choice. She stepped up on the windowsill and closed her eyes before letting herself topple out of the window. She dropped through the air for only a fraction of a second before she felt herself hit something solid. Fear cut through her that she had landed on the ground on her back despite trying to right herself and she remained still, not wanting to feel the pain that she expected would be there in a matter of moments. It took a few beats for her to realize that she was moving and that what she had hit wasn't the ground, but arms.

She opened her eyes and immediately felt the breath catch in her throat. Aubrey was so stunned by the face of the man who was carrying her that she couldn't even move, couldn't bring herself to try to get free of his grasp. He had been carrying her for several seconds, running away from the building, before she realized that she didn't even know if Jonah had made it out of the factory safely. She looked behind them and saw that he was running after them, Ilya and Mordecai close behind. That was enough to snap her thoughts into reality and she wriggled until she felt her feet touch the ground. Without hesitating, knowing that they couldn't afford even a second of lost time, she continued to run. The group came together, tightening to one another as if it could afford them some type of protection. Sirens suddenly sliced through the air and when she glanced behind them again she could see the black cloaked figures of the Valdicians starting to seep out of the factory. They emerged from doors, they slipped from cracked windows, they seemed to rise up from the ground.

Aubrey didn't want to take her eyes off them, but she needed to look ahead. She knew what they were capable of. She knew that in an instant they could have her under their control without even being close enough to touch them. They were only steps away. She felt something tugging on her and realized that she was being pulled backward. She reached out and grasped onto Jonah, then saw Ilya drop to her knees, her fingers digging into the ground as she clawed her way back toward them, fighting with everything in her to resist the pull of the Valdician minds behind her. Aubrey had left the ground and was looking down on the group, screaming for Jonah, when she saw both human men take bows from harnesses that she hadn't even noticed strapped to their backs and withdraw arrows from the same harnesses. In seconds they had shot the arrows and Aubrey watched as what looked like singular missiles split in the air and became several so that the arrows showered down on the Valdicians. She heard a bloodcurdling scream come from several of the creatures that were following them.

As quickly as she had felt herself rising, she felt herself falling and crashed into the ground, landing on top of Ilya. She scrambled up, scared that she had hurt the woman or the baby that she was carrying, and reached down to help her, only then realizing that she wasn't being dragged backward anymore. Both men turned slightly and shot off more arrows, repeating the procedure once more. Each time resulted in more screams and the throng pushed back. Aubrey took Ilya's hand and they continued to run, following the men through the fence and into the woods. She thought that they would run toward the van they had brought, but soon realized that they were running in a different direction. She followed without questioning, knowing that hesitation would only be dangerous. Soon they were at another vehicle, this one more intimidating looking than the van, and they piled into it.

When the doors slammed behind them, Aubrey turned toward Jonah, her eyes tracing the harness that he wore on his back. It was then that she realized that he was wearing different, though similar, clothing than she had seen him in earlier. Her eyes lifted to his face and her heart began to beat faster in her chest as she noticed changes and a long scar long healed along the side of his cheek. He reached for her, his fingertips resting on her palm. He felt the same and

Aubrey felt comfort blend with the confusion that she was feeling. Jonah nodded slightly toward the front of the car and Aubrey turned to see the man who had caught her behind the wheel, driving them out of the woods.

"Frederick, this is Aubrey. Aubrey, this is..."

"My father."

5

The hairs on the back of Mhavrych's neck stood up when he saw Ryan walk into the office. He had witnessed his interactions with Eden a few times in the couple of weeks that he had been posing as an administrative assistant in the laboratory so that he could watch them. He saw her body tense and the expression on her face become uncomfortable. It happened every time her boss was near. It was evident that he made her incredibly uncomfortable and on more than one occasion Mhavrych had heard her mutter a polite but insistent reminder to keep his hands to himself. This almost always resulted in him giving her an assignment far more suited for the graduate students who hoped for credits and recommendations in exchange for doing the grudge work throughout the laboratory.

"Ms. Baines, I have a new assignment for you."

She leaned back in her desk chair and Ryan settled in the chair across from her. Mhavrych subtly shifted so that he could move closer to them and listen to their conversation. He wondered if this is what he had been waiting for. He came back through the streams to bring himself to Earth before Eden had left for Uoria. When he first arrived he'd gotten a glimpse of Kendra and knew that he was in the right place. A simple note had told him to wait until she left, and Mhavrych had been posing within the laboratory since then, monitoring their interactions, and waiting for the moment when Eden would climb onto the ship to head on her mission. He didn't know what he was meant to learn from watching, and he wished that he could stop her, but he knew that if he did the consequences would be far worse than anything she had seen on the planet. He had to remind himself that she, along with the other women, had been instrumental in as far as they had come in their fight against Ryan, the Valdicians, and the Klimnu.

"You're going on a trip."

Out of the corner of his eye, Mhavrych noticed Eden's eyebrows lift slightly in surprise.

"Where to?"

"Uoria."

Eden immediately looked nervous and her eyes shifted from side to side. Mhavrych stilled and turned his attention back to the slides that he was aimlessly sifting through, hoping that she didn't notice his presence any more than she usually did. Eden was intense and cold, not cruel or vicious, but also not immediately welcoming. Mhavrych had exchanged fewer than ten words with her in the entire time he was in the laboratory and he doubted that when he returned to Uoria she would have any memory of him even being there. That was what he wanted. He didn't want to interfere with anything that he was watching. Not yet, anyway. There may come a time when he needed to step in, to change something, to prepare for what would happen in what was both the future and the past. He hoped he would recognize it when it happened. But for now, he was only there to watch.

"What for?"

It was obvious that Eden was hesitant at the idea of traveling to the planet that was still considered wild and fairly unknown. Though humans had visited regularly for some time, those visits had stopped decades before with little explanation. The majority of people on earth now only knew the stories of the vicious, bloodthirsty Warriors who called Uoria home. Most would be hesitant to even visit the planet, much less attempt to interact with them on a scientific level. Mhavrych had heard the beginnings of conversations about the exchange program that exists between the University and the Denynso, but Ryan had made no mention that sending Eden there had anything to do with that program.

"We need to learn more about them, what's in their blood," Ryan replied.

His voice was casual, almost dismisses as if he was making a no acknowledgment of the danger he was putting Eden in simply by making the request. Mhavrych could see in Eden's face that hearing that assignment was both startling and terrifying. She gasped, her hands falling from where they had been clasped on her stomach as she leaned back. Her chair righted, and she leaned slightly closer to Ryan, not seeming to want to get close to him, but wanting to lower her voice. Mhavrych wondered if maybe she had noticed that he was there, if she wanted to keep him from hearing what she was saying to protect herself from this unknown, strange assistant who appeared without recommendation and had to talk himself into the position while knowing little about the work they were doing, potentially going to the department head and revealing what he had heard them discussing.

"You know that's against the rules, Ryan."

It had already been documented that the Denynso Warriors had willingly submitted to some testing by human scientists years before and had relented to continue the testing of the samples that those scientists had brought back, with the understanding they were to never attempt to access or test the warrior blood. Now that the samples that had been collected decades before were largely gone, it made sense that further research would require more contact and the collection of other samples, possibly testing on live subjects, but that wasn't what Ryan was suggesting. The brilliant, revered, and often feared scientist was telling Eden that he needed her to do something that was directly against the policies and agreements that had been made between the two species. It wasn't just unethical. It was dangerous. The few scientists who had decided that their curiosity about the blood of the Warriors was too much to comply with the restrictions had never returned to Earth. The Denynso gave no explanation for what had happened to them. Their official response was simply that the king and queen made their rules and had been clear about them, and those scientists had breached them.

He shrugged, his expression showing that he was unfazed by her reaction and didn't care if she felt unsure or even afraid to follow through with what he was telling her to do.

"You're sneaky enough and no one pays much attention to you. We need to know what makes them so powerful," he said.

It was an insult disguised as a compliment, but Eden wasn't falling for it. Mhavrych could see her body shudder.

"But..." she started weakly, her voice so low that Mhavrych didn't even know if the scientist had heard her.

Ryan didn't seem to care even if he did. He leaned forward to rest his arms on the desk and look at her with a smug expression on his face. One that said he knew she was largely at his mercy. After all, he was the powerful lead scientist of the laboratory, one with absolute control over research and experiments that were done throughout this section of the University. He was often at odds with the other lead scientists who controlled other research and projects in other departments of the lab, but there was rarely a question of his intelligence or vision. In the end, Eden, though brilliant and vital in how his work turned out, was merely his assistant. She was obligated to do as he instructed.

"Oh, and preferably the blood from their strongest warrior is what you need to get. You've heard of him, right?"

There was an oily thread through Ryan's voice, an arrogance that made Mhavrych's jaw tighten. He didn't know Eden well. But he had heard of what she had done since being on Uoria and the incredible transformation that she had undergone when she became Denynso rather than human after a healing. He had a sense of respect for who she was going to become once she left this office and he had the sense of duty to defend her as a member of the rebellion. Again, he had to remind himself that he couldn't interfere. He was here only to learn, to understand how everything unfolded, so he knew where to go next.

"You know I won't do that."

Her voice sounded as though she had gotten herself under control and she was adamant, determined that he wasn't going to push her into something that she knew was not only ethically and morally irresponsible and could put her career in jeopardy, but also something that could threaten her life. Ryan was unmoved. He shrugged and stood.

"Then your job is as good as gone and so will your reputation. You'll never work again. Not in this field" He spun on his heel and looked over his shoulder. "Might as well practice saying, 'Do you want fries with that?' because that's the only work you'll ever get. You know how much we need this information."

In an instant, he had gone from being arrogant and dismissive to being angry and forceful, and it affected Eden. His eyes burned into her and when he turned to walk away, Mhavrych could see her body sag slightly as she relented to what she knew was a situation she truly had no choice in if she wanted to protect all that she had worked so hard to achieve.

"Wait," Eden said and sighed. "I'll do it."

Mhavrych started for the door to the office, wanting to get out before Ryan did so that he could follow the scientist after he left. He saw the smile on Ryan's face and immediately knew that Eden had been right in her assessment that the danger is what her boss intended for her all along. He knew once he sent her to Uoria with the intention of gathering the blood of Pyra, the fiercest and most feared warrior in the galaxy, she would never return, and that was exactly what he wanted. They wouldn't hesitate to kill her. Ryan wanted to get rid of her. He knew she was a threat to him. Though Mhavrych had heard that Eden thought Ryan sent her on this mission largely because she had spurned his advances so many times, he knew that wasn't really the case. Though that might be an extra perk to getting Eden out of the laboratory and sending her to the certain death he was sure awaited her, it wasn't the main motivation. There was something else driving him.

He wanted her gone so that she didn't stand in his way.

"Good, I knew you'd see it my way. You need to be ready at four a.m."

Mhavrych kept his back to the door of the office until he heard Ryan leave and then turned to follow him down the hallway. The scientist had left the door open and as he passed Mhavrych could see Eden working frantically on her computer. The look of fear was gone from her face, replaced by a smile that bordered on smug. He didn't know what she was doing, and he couldn't take the time to continue to watch her. He needed to follow Ryan.

Mhavrych rushed down the hallway before he could lose the sound of the scientist's footsteps. They made their way through the building until they reached one of the labs. He walked inside and put on a white lab coat that was hanging from a hook on the wall. He paused and turned toward the door, catching sight of Mhavrych.

"What are you doing?" he asked. "Who are you?"

It confirmed that Ryan paid such little attention to the people around him, feeling that he was the most important figure in any situation, that he didn't even recognize the face of a man who had been in his lab daily for weeks. The thought of how much time had passed was strange to Mhavrych. Though he felt that he had been away for so long, adjusting to the ways of Earth with help from those he had encountered, he also knew that when he returned to his own time it would have been only a matter of moments since he would have been gone. When Lucian showed him the rocks, let him hear what they whispered, and he discovered that though the Eteri man didn't really know what he had found but that he could manipulate the streams, traveling to any moment he pleased with the portals, Mhavrych knew that he was a step closer in bringing this to an end.

It wasn't as simple as just changing the things that had gone wrong. He couldn't just go back to the moments when things happened and prevent them from happening. Killing Ryan now would solve nothing. Doing that would mean leaving those he had tortured and imprisoned helpless. It would also mean never resolving how it all began. He had to find those links to really understand how it all connected. Though these were moments he couldn't change, events that he couldn't stop from happening because they would mean altering everything that had come after, they were ways he could prevent the further destruction that was promised.

"I'm an assistant," Mhavrych said. "I was just checking to see if you needed any help with anything."

He hated offering even a modicum of service to Ryan, but it was his only choice.

"No, I don't need anything," Ryan said sharply.

Mhavrych started to turn, but then heard Ryan again.

"Wait."

"Yes?"

"Actually, yes. Maybe I could use your help. What level of authorization do you have?"

It was a question that Mhavrych hadn't been asked yet. He had been given credentials when he got the position, but the access chip that he had in his pocket had been given to him by its original owner to allow him easier movement throughout the laboratory when he had the opportunity. He had never been briefed on the different levels of authorization and which he would have, which led him to believe that he was at the very bottom along with the other nameless, faceless drudges who did so much of the work and got none of the recognition.

"I am an administrative assistant," he said.

From the description of the position he had been given it was different from the role of the same title in the offices, but similar. Essentially it was his responsibility to do anything and everything that was asked of him so the more important members of the research teams didn't have to.

Ryan nodded, his expression thoughtful. His eyes moved up and down Mhavrych as if evaluating him, scrutinizing him. Finally, a hint of a smile came to his lips.

"That will do just fine. Come with me."

He led Mhavrych through the lab and a honeycomb of rooms behind it before descending stairs into a section of the building that Mhavrych had yet to enter. This section didn't utilize access chips. Rather, he input a code into a keypad beside the door and waited until the sound of a heavy lock within the mechanism released before pressing the latch and opening the door. Mhavrych noticed that he had done nothing to conceal the code that he had put in and had given no indications that Mhavrych wasn't supposed to talk about this area or what they were going to do to anyone. This wasn't reassuring. Instead, it made Mhavrych feel as though Ryan didn't think he needed to conceal this information or give any warnings because he had no concern that the lowly assistant now following him into the strange section of the building would have any opportunity to use the details later.

Mhavrych let his eyes scan every surface he could as they walked through the rooms, chronicling everything that he saw, making a record of it in his mind. He wanted to remember everything. Even if he didn't know why or how he was going to use the information later, he wanted to have it. Finally, they reached another door and Ryan put in another code, this one different from the first. Mhavrych stepped through the door first and found himself in a round room. He walked into the center of it and stood beside what looked like a round, dark blue cushioned ottoman. Ryan came in and pressed a button on the wall.

Lights burst on along the curved walls, illuminating what looked like smaller rooms separated from the center area with glass doors. Each had a bench attached to the wall at the back and what appeared to be a long tubular light positioned on one side. Mhavrych looked at Ryan.

"What are those?" he asked.

"Observation chambers," he said. "They are for an experiment that I've been working on."

"I haven't heard of any type of experiment with chambers like these," Mhavrych pointed out.

Ryan smiled.

"Ah. Well, that's because it is a confidential experiment that isn't under the regulation of the University. It is my private work."

Mhavrych nodded.

"What do you need me to do?"

"If you could please step into one of the chambers," Ryan said. "I'm going to close the door. You will then hear a series of sounds and experience a series of other sensory stimulation. Please just react to them however comes naturally. Feel free to take a moment to get acquainted with the chamber before we get started."

Feeling unsure but knowing that this was the closest he had yet gotten to learning about Ryan and his experiments before Eden left, Mhavrych walked into one of the chambers. Ryan followed him and secured the glass door closed. Mhavrych looked around and quickly realized that he was sealed in. There was no space between the top of the glass and the ceiling and he was completely separated from the chambers on either side of him. As Ryan had suggested, he took a few moments to get himself used to the space. He looked at the bench which appeared to be nothing but a piece of thick white plastic. He then looked at the light and noticed a narrow rectangular bar beside it.

"Are you ready?" Ryan asked.

Mhavrych looked through the glass at the scientist and nodded. Ryan walked over to a panel positioned on the wall of the room and hit a button. Immediately the glass chamber filled with a low tone that felt like it was vibrating in Mhavrych's chest. It wasn't unpleasant, but he also didn't know how to react to it. A second later the sound changed to a high note and Mhavrych twisted his head against the discomfort it caused, as if trying to escape it. The tone quickly changed to a soft fluttering sound followed by a trickle like water. The changing sounds continued for several minutes before Mhavrych realized that the temperature in the chamber had shifted. He felt a stinging hot on his skin that was suddenly replaced by intense cold. A rush of air hit him and then the floor beneath his feet started to shake, throwing him off balance until he stumbled back and landed sitting on the bench at the back of the chamber. He was starting to feel confused and unnerved, but when he reached for the door he realized that there was no way to open it from inside the chamber.

The smell of flowers filled the space, quickly followed by dirt, then something salty and sharp. Finally, his lungs were overtaken by a thick, sickly sweet odor that brought back a rush of memories that Mhavrych never wanted to experience again. He was starting to panic, to feel overwhelmed by the smell and the cold air, when suddenly it all stopped. The chamber went still. All traces of the smells, sounds, and movement were gone. Mhavrych stared out of the glass door, searching for Ryan, wondering if he was going to just walk up and open the door. But he didn't. Instead, he saw Ryan type something into a small tablet that he drew from his pocket, put it back in, and walk out of the room, turning off the lights as he went.

Mhavrych was plunged into complete darkness. He stood still for a few seconds, waiting for something to happen, then realized that he was alone. Ryan hadn't returned to the room and there was no indication that anyone else might be there. He remembered the light on the wall and the small rectangular piece beside it. He stretched out his hand until he felt the wall of the chamber and ran his fingertips along the smooth surface until he felt the rectangular piece that he assumed was a light switch. He pressed it and the light tube turned on, filling the chamber with a blue glow. There was some relief of having the light on, but it still did nothing for him. There was no way to open the door, no way to get out of the chamber. He felt along the sides, pressing against them, hoping that it would release.

When it didn't, Mhavrych started feeling along the walls of the chamber, running his palms across them to feel for any changes in the surface that might indicate another way that he could get out of the space. He didn't know what Ryan's intentions had been putting him in here. He hadn't specified what the experiments were for or what he was observing in the chamber, and now that he was not in the room Mhavrych didn't know what he planned to do next. Climbing up onto the bench, Mhavrych ran his hands along the top of the back wall and then leaned so that he could feel the top of the other walls as far as he could reach.

After several minutes he realized that he was starting to feel strange. He was getting lightheaded and it was harder to focus. He felt like he was no longer sure of what he had been doing and didn't know what he was supposed to do next. His lungs were starting to burn and no matter how much he struggled, he didn't feel as though he was able to get enough air into them. His body was starting to feel weaker and he didn't feel like he was able to hold himself up. Dropping down from the bench, he sat hard onto it. The burning in his lungs worsened and spots started to dance in front of his eyes. His mind was blurred, unable to grasp anything that was happening. He couldn't remember how he had gotten in there or what he was supposed to be doing. All he wanted to do was sleep.

Mhavrych felt his muscles weaken further until he wasn't able to hold himself up on the bench. He slipped down, soon finding himself sitting on the floor of the chamber with his head dropped back. His eyes stared blankly at the ceiling, trying to process what he was seeing, anything. A sound came from beyond the chamber, but he didn't know how to react. He heard what he thought might be the door slam and thought that someone might be coming. He struggled with his mind, fighting the memories forward, until he remembered how he had gotten to the chamber. Maybe the sound was Ryan coming back for him. Mhavrych dropped over to his side and tried to pull himself toward the door, but he felt like there was no breath getting into his lungs and his muscles had no strength. A figure appeared at the door, but he could only see the feet. They weren't the heavy dark shoes and black pants that Ryan had been wearing. Instead, they were small and wrapped in delicate gold shoes. Something shimmered slightly as the feet moved to the side and he heard the door open.

Hands grasped him, and he felt himself getting pulled along the floor of the chamber. His head and shoulders slipped out, dropping down the side of the low platform until he lay on the floor again. As soon as his head hit the floor, Mhavrych felt the air rushing back into his lungs. His mind cleared and the stinging on his skin dissipated. As he started to feel normal again, he opened his eyes and saw a small, beautiful woman standing over him. His mind swam for another few seconds, then cleared and he realized who he was looking at.

"Kendra," he murmured.

"Shhhh," she said, stroking his face. "You're going to be alright. It's all alright now. We need to hurry, though."

"Hurry?"

"He's going to be coming back."

"Who?"

"Ryan," Kendra said insistently, pulling on him now, trying to get him to his feet. "He brought you here to test a technology that he created. If he finds the chamber empty, it will ruin everything."

"What are we going to do?"

A sad look crossed Kendra's eyes and she guided him across the room to a shadowy area not touched by the glow still coming from the chamber that Mhavrych had been in. She touched the light inside and Mhavrych recoiled when he saw a body slumped on the floor.

"Who is that?" he asked.

"A hybrid," Kendra said sadly. "He was lost in the experiments. There's nothing that can help him now, but he can help us."

"What do you mean?"

"We need to get him inside the chamber."

"But Ryan will notice," Mhavrych argued. "He doesn't look like me and we're wearing different clothing."

Kendra's eyes rose to his and Mhavrych knew what she was thinking.

"Hurry," she said. "He'll be coming back. Hurry. We only have a few seconds more."

Mhavrych didn't know what she meant by that, but he rushed to strip off his clothes while Kendra carefully removed what the hybrid man had been wearing when he died. Mhavrych's stomach turned when she offered the clothing to him and took the pile that she offered him. He pulled the clothing on while she dressed the hybrid in his clothes. Together they scooped him up and brought him over to the chamber. Mhavrych didn't want to get near the chamber again, but he quickly approached it, put the body inside, and then slammed the door closed.

"But we still don't look similar enough for Ryan not to recognize that that isn't me," Mhavrych said. "The clothing isn't going to be enough to convince him."

"Just wait," Kendra said. "Be patient."

Moments before she had been pushing him, rushing him and telling him to hurry. Now she was telling him to be patient. She took his hand and pulled him back a few feet so that they stood behind the cushioned ottoman.

"What are we waiting for?"

"Wait."

Seconds later there was an instant of blinding flash as flames filled the chamber. When they disappeared, the body had been severely singed, with only a few details still visible. Some of Mhavrych's clothing was recognizable, but there was enough damage to the body that it couldn't be identified. A sick feeling flooded Mhavrych and he let the feeling of Kendra's hand guide him through the room and out of the door that Ryan had brought him through. They rushed back through the honeycomb of rooms and he followed her as she ducked into a small storage room.

"What was that?" he asked.

"He is experimenting with a technology that kills by removing oxygen from the air and draws nutrients out of the body."

"Why did we have to watch that?"

"No one deserves to be forgotten."

Mhavrych nodded, the words settling heavily in his chest.

"How can Ryan get away with that? How can he kill people like that and no one knows?"

"He can do what people don't know about," she said. "I suppose that it's good for him that he doesn't have security cameras in that section of the laboratory."

Before Mhavrych could say anything else, Kendra leaned forward and touched a soft kiss to his lips, then brought her mouth to his ear, sweeping her hand over his eyes so that he would close them.

"Find me," she whispered.

Her hand fell away and he heard the door to the storage room close. He opened his eyes and looked out of the door. Kendra was gone.

Security cameras. Why would she mention security cameras?

6

———

Jonah felt like he couldn't speak as the car drove away from the factory. Aubrey's revelation sat like a rock in his stomach and he didn't know what he was supposed to think or what to say. Her father? What did she mean that Frederick was her father? It didn't make any sense. When the older man brought him out of the factory Jonah had trusted him because he said that he knew Nana. Though it seemed strange and he didn't understand the man's sudden appearance at the factory or the fact that he wanted him to leave without Aubrey, it had been his promise of a connection with Nana and the insistence that they didn't have the time to hesitate or even to think that made Jonah listen to him. What had happened after was something that Jonah could never have expected, but this had thrown him even further, confused him even more, made him feel even more like he was completely out of control.

He had been so happy to see Aubrey. She didn't know what he had been through or how long it had really been since he had been able to hold her in his arms. He knew that to her it had only been a matter of less than an hour since they had parted ways in the basement, but to Jonah, it had been years. They had timed their return to the factory precisely, taking the time to first go to the school to meet with Linnea and gather the supplies and information that they needed to ensure that they were completely ready before going to the factory. It was critical that they entered at just the right moment. They couldn't go in too soon and potentially risk overlapping their streams in a way that could be dangerous to all of them, but they also couldn't wait too long and leave Aubrey and the others at serious risk. Through all his preparation and all that he had gone through, however, nothing braced him for those two words that Aubrey had just said.

How could Frederick not have told him? In all that they had gone through together, in the years that they had spent traveling, fighting, researching. Through all they had done to get them ready for this moment and for the work that still lay ahead. Through all of that, never had he mentioned that he had any relationship to Aubrey, much less that he was her father.

They had all fallen silent after the revelation and they drove along tensely as if each was lost in their own thoughts and unwilling to compromise the sanctity of the stillness or the confidentiality of their own minds. Even if they did, Jonah didn't know what to say. He had already been trying to come up with how he was going to explain to her what had happened. It was already going to be incredibly difficult to tell her what had happened after she left the basement and what was still lying ahead for them. Now that was out of his mind. It didn't matter what she thought of what he had done. What mattered was the questions of why. Why didn't she tell him who her father was? Did she even know? Why hadn't Frederick told him that he was Aubrey's father? Where was her mother? Why didn't Nana tell Aubrey what her parents did and why they weren't around? Why had Frederick chosen this moment to resurface rather than sooner? How did he even know to come?

The questions were filling his mind so completely that Jonah barely recognized that the car was slowing and then stopped. He heard the slamming of the front door and it brought his attention away from the place in the dark blue carpeting on the floor of the car that he had been staring at since they left the factory. He looked around, noticing that it was inky black outside of the car. They were outside of a large building and it took a few seconds for Jonah to process the fact that they had arrived at a hotel. He didn't know how long it had been since they left the factory or where they were, and even as everyone else around him was getting out of the car, he stayed in place. It was as if the impact of everything he had experienced and everything that was still to come had suddenly hit him and he didn't know how to get through the next moment

The door beside him opened and he turned to see Aubrey looking in at him. They stared at each other for a few seconds in silence.

"Come on inside," she finally said. "We all need to get some sleep."

"There's a lot that we need to talk about."

"In the morning, Jonah. We need to get some rest."

Jonah shook his head.

"No. We need to talk. I need to understand all of this."

"None of us have the energy to go through all of it tonight. We've been through so much already. We need to rest and then we can talk through it when we have a clear mind."

She said it as though she was trying to push away the thought of anything that he wanted to talk about. She was pulling away from it, trying to ignore it, trying to pretend as though none of it had happened or was happening and that she didn't need to acknowledge it.

"Aubrey, you just told me that a man I thought I knew is your father. How am I supposed to just ignore that? Aren't you curious at all? Don't you want to know how I met him or why he's here? Haven't you noticed that I look different?"

He felt almost desperate. He couldn't understand why she was so dismissive, how she could just push it all aside and not feel the way that he was. Aubrey's eyes flashed, and her jaw tightened.

"Of course, I'm curious. Of course, I want to know all of that. Of course, I've noticed. But it scares the hell out of me and I just can't deal with it right now. I'm exhausted and I need to sleep. I just want to go to sleep. I will have to face it all tomorrow and I know that there's nothing that I can do about that, but for now, I don't. For now, I can go into that hotel, take the longest, hottest shower that I have ever taken, and then go to sleep. Are you going to come with me, or are you going to stay here in the car?"

He had never seen her like this. Jonah didn't know how he should process the change that he was seeing in her. He had missed her so much. For the years that he had been gone from her, he had felt like there was a part of him missing, like someone had taken his heart out. He had hoped that when he got to see her again he would have the opportunity to savor holding her in his arms again. Though she wouldn't have felt their separation and wouldn't know the pain that he had gone through, he wanted to embrace her, to show her how much he loved her, to make sure that she knew that she was on his mind every single day, every moment of the day, no matter what he was going through. No matter what he was doing or what he was facing during those years, she was always there in his thoughts. She never left his mind and he longed for her with every beat of his heart.

Now, though, she looked tired, frustrated, and even angry. She didn't feel the love that he wanted to show her, or even the urge to understand what they had found themselves. Jonah had learned so much in the time that he had spent with Frederick and had an even greater sense of urgency about all that they needed to do, but now that he was here with Aubrey, alone for the first time in so long, he felt like he knew less than he ever had.

"I don't know what I'm supposed to do now," he said.

"Come inside with me. Go to sleep."

Jonah finally nodded and climbed out of the car. He walked alongside Aubrey across the nearly empty parking lot toward the brightly glowing glass doors that led into the lobby of the hotel. Her hand brushed his and he took it, tightly intertwining their fingers to create the connection that he had been searching for since he first saw her running through the hall of the factory and reached out to grab her. For those moments as they walked through the night it felt almost as though all was normal again. He could just enjoy the feeling of her hand in his, their skin together, and know that things were going to be alright.

They stepped through the doors and into the bright lobby. Jonah winced slightly as the light hit his eyes and he again wondered how long he had been in the car. Wondered if he had fallen asleep or if he had just spent the trip staring, unable to keep himself present in the moment as his mind went to work untangling the thoughts, questions, and memories that were clashing inside. Frederick was standing near an elevator to the far side of the lobby and as they walked by the front desk Jonah noticed the man standing behind it lift his eyes and watch them. He looked curious and unnerved, as if he had noticed the unusual assortment of people that had just walked through the lobby. Jonah could only assume that this hotel didn't get a tremendous amount of business thanks to its location seemingly away from everything else, and that few people showed up in the middle of the night.

They walked to Frederick, who opened the elevator as they approached. They rode up two floors in silence and then made their way down the corridor. It suddenly occurred to Jonah how long it had been since he had been in a hotel. During the years that he had been traveling with Frederick, they had stayed in homes, camped, found shelter in abandoned buildings they came across. He hadn't been in a hotel since before he left for the Nyx 23 mission. Yet nothing seemed to have changed. It was a strange realization. The surroundings were exactly as he remembered. There was so much that was different about Earth now that he had returned from the time he had spent on Uoria. Though he had only had conscious memory of just over 15 years of that time, the further he explored and the more he experienced, the more evident it was just how long his absence really was. The changes were extensive, the progress breathtaking. But here in this hotel, time had stopped. Everything seemed just as it had in the hotel that he stayed in before he left. The walls looked so similar, with a somewhat unbalanced combination of textured paint and wallpaper in a mix of cream, dusty blue, and mauve that seemed a popular choice among hotels. The carpet felt like the same thick, dense texture that he remembered and when he looked down at it Jonah saw that it had the swirling pattern that gave the impression of the carpet being lush and thick even though it was industrial in order to make it easy to clean.

What struck him the most, however, was the smell. As they walked down the quiet, cold hallway, Jonah could remember the smell of the hotel that he stayed in before getting onboard the StarCity. It was the same smell as this hotel, something fresh and clean, but completely unique to hotels. In front of him, Frederick stopped in front of a door and Jonah's mind snapped back into the current moment. It seemed ridiculous that he had gotten so wrapped up in the experience of walking down the hallway of the hotel, that of all the things he had experienced since coming back to Earth, that was what had struck him the most. Yet it was reassuring in a way, comforting in its consistency and predictability. He was willing to give in to the superficial reality of focusing on these details. He was happy to give himself over to something with little impact, little meaning to the rest of the world, just so that he could feel like he had some control and some sense of stability as everything else tilted and twirled around him. If he could put himself back into that feeling before he got onto the ship, he could remind himself of a time when none of this had happened. He could remind himself of a time when he cared only about getting on the ship and going to a planet that was being misused so he could save the tormented and imprisoned who were on it.

He never would have believed that he wouldn't return to Earth in the few months that they thought it would take. He never would have believed how much more they would uncover or what they would go through just to finish what they started.

Now he just hoped that they would have a chance.

Frederick opened the door to the room and they walked through. Jonah walked in and noticed Ilya, Mordecai, Willow, and Gannon sitting on the long couch and two over-stuffed chairs positioned around a low table in the center of what looked like a living area. It was the first moment that he realized that Willow and Gannon hadn't been in the car with them when they were coming from the factory. He wondered how they had gotten there, but he didn't have the energy to ask. He put down the bag that he had carried from the car and filled a cup from the nearby counter with hot coffee, swallowing it so fast it burned his throat. When he put the cup down, he looked at Frederick.

"Where am I sleeping?" he asked, trying to withhold the anger that he was feeling.

Jonah hated that he was feeling so angry toward the man who he had learned to trust and rely on so much. He knew there had to be a reason that he hadn't been forthcoming with him. There had to be an explanation for not telling him everything that he needed to know. Yet he felt betrayed by him. In the back of his mind, he also felt that Aubrey had been betrayed. By the way her voice sounded when she made the declaration that Frederick was her father Jonah could tell that she didn't know what he had been doing. She had no idea who he really was or what had brought him away from her all those times, keeping him from seeing her for years. He had seen the pain in her eyes and confusion on her face. He knew how much it had shocked her when she saw him, but at the same time Jonah couldn't help but wonder how she couldn't know anything. She had to have. There had to be some kind of indication, something that would tell her that her family was far more than just their wealth.

"Jonah..." Frederick started.

"I need to get some sleep," he said.

He had just argued with Aubrey when she said the same thing, wanting to talk, but now that he was facing them, Jonah wanted to get out of the room. As much as the questions were filling his mind and digging through his thoughts, he no longer wanted to face them. Not yet. For now, he needed to continue to think that everything was as it had been and the plans that they had laid could remain as they were. Frederick didn't respond, and Jonah turned away from the group to head through one of the three doors that were to the sides of the living area. He stepped through and was startled to see that Aubrey was inside. He hadn't noticed that she had walked in there, and yet he must have because he had chosen that one to go into rather than any of the others.

Aubrey turned to look at him from the small suitcase that was set on the bed.

"These are my clothes," she said softly.

Jonah nodded as he walked up to the bed and put his own bag down on it. He opened it and pulled out a pair of pajamas.

"I know," he said. "I brought it."

"But it isn't my suitcase. I mean, not the one that I brought when we left for the factory."

"I know," he said. "That one was in the other car and I didn't know if it was going to make it here. I wanted to make sure that you had what you needed when I came for you, so I had that one packed for you."

"By who?"

"Linnea," he said.

"Linnea?" Aubrey sounded surprised. "Why? I mean...how? She didn't come with us. You were already in the factory."

"I wasn't there when I asked her."

"I don't understand."

"I know you don't."

Jonah took his clothes and brought them into the bathroom so that he could shower before getting dressed. By the time that he came out, Aubrey was in her nightgown and curled up in the bed, her eyes closed. Jonah turned off the lamp and slipped under the blankets with her. The muscles and joints throughout his body relaxed into the mattress despite the tension that was coursing through him. His body felt more comfortable than he had in as long as he could remember and the combination of that comfort and the feeling of the warmth of Aubrey's body radiating toward his instantly made Jonah start to drift to sleep.

"Why do you look different?"

Aubrey's voice was soft and cautious in the dark and for a moment Jonah wasn't sure he had actually heard her say anything and that it wasn't the beginning of a dream.

"Hmmm?" he said, more a groan of acknowledgment than any real words so that if she hadn't actually spoken to him he would have less of a chance of waking her up with his response.

"Why do you look so different?" she asked. "You don't look the same."

Jonah's heart thudded in his chest and he rolled over so that he was on his side facing Aubrey. She turned to face him as well, so their faces were just inches apart. He could feel her breath brushing across his skin and hear it as it moved in and out of her lungs. It was reassuring, and he felt the anger that had built inside of him start to seep away. He was too happy to be back so close to her that he could reach out and touch her to be angry. He had already been through too much to be upset.

"What looks different?" he asked, knowing how much he had changed but also wanting to hear it from her so that he could understand what she was seeing and how she was internalizing it.

"You're wearing different clothes than you were when you were in the basement," she said.

Jonah let out a brief, involuntary laugh.

"My clothes?" he asked. "That's what you noticed about me?"

He could hear the voices of the rest of the group still in the other room, so he kept his voice lower. He didn't want them listening. Though they were only talking about something that he knew they would all discuss come morning, he still felt protective of the conversation that they were having. It was the closest thing that he'd had to privacy with Aubrey for so long that he didn't want to share any of it with anyone else. Until they were all in the same room talking about all that was unfolding, this was his time to talk only with her.

"No," she said. "I noticed more. I just didn't want to..."

Jonah slid a little closer to her and shook his head.

"It's alright," he said. "I know that I look different. I should. It's been years since you've seen me."

Aubrey looked startled.

"What?" she asked. "What do you mean it's been years since I've seen you? You were in the basement when I walked out of it. You were right there. I left and heard Ryan shouting for Ilya --"

"And you went after him and shouted for him to come get you and started running through the factory. You shined your lightstick on him to distract him from going after them but then you put it in your pocket so that it wouldn't be bright enough for you to really call attention to yourself while you were going down the halls and up and down the stairs. You didn't know where the Valdicians were and you didn't know what was going to happen if they found you, so you just ran through the dark."

Aubrey nodded.

"Yes," she said softly. "How did you know that?"

"I was there," Jonah said. "I watched it happen."

"But how did you get out of the basement fast enough to be there? And how did I not see you running after me?"

"Because I didn't come out of the basement."

"I don't understand."

Jonah took a breath. He had always known that he was going to have to have this conversation, but he thought he was going to have Frederick right there with him to help him through it. Now he was going to have to come up with the words himself and just hope that he chose the right ones so that he was able to tell her all that he had done and all that they still needed to do. It seemed strange to feel so unsure preparing to tell her about his movements through years that had already passed. He came from a century before, had technically lived through many more years than his lifespan should have allowed him. But this was different. When he lived those years, it was because of the Covra and the toxin that they had pumped into his body along with all the other members of Nyx 23. He hadn't really lived those years and he had done nothing to move through them.

With Frederick, though, he had. Along with Frederick, he had jumped through spans of time that for the first months that he was away from the factory left him feeling dizzy and confused. He took to writing out where and when they had gone and what they had done so he could keep track and ensure that he always knew where he was in the timeline of his past so he didn't overlap. Now that his timeline had reconciled, and he had returned to his own line of progress, he didn't have to worry about the potential dangers of encountering himself unwittingly, but he did have to acknowledge the changes that had come over him in the time since Frederick brought him out of the factory.

The years had changed him. Though his grasp on how the moments, days, and years worked when he was moving through them still felt unsure, Jonah knew that he didn't look exactly the same as he had when he left. His face was older now, if only slightly, and the scar that stretched down the side of his cheek marked him with a reminder of what he endured and what he accomplished. Skirting carefully around discussing Frederick as anything more than the man who had come for him, Jonah told Aubrey all that had happened and what he had learned. The complexity of Ryan and the Valdicians started to fall open in front of her, but there were still gaps, there were still questions, just as there were for him. That was why they needed to come back now. They needed her. They needed Ilya and Mordecai. They needed to keep them from Ryan.

THEY TALKED until the sun was starting to come up and then finally drifted to sleep, but Jonah could only rest for a few hours. He was soon awake and pacing around the living room when Frederick came out of one of the other bedrooms. His eyes met Frederick's and there was an unspoken exchange. The older man looked as though he knew that this moment would come and had been dreading it. He didn't seem to know what to say or how to resolve the tension that now existed between the two that had come to lean on each other.

"Why didn't you tell me?" Jonah finally asked. "How could you not tell me?"

Frederick sighed and took a few more steps toward Jonah.

"I couldn't, Jonah. I need you to trust me when I tell you that I didn't mean to deceive you. I didn't want to lie to you or to make you think that I was trying to keep something from you. That wasn't my intention. I just knew that there was no way that I could explain it to you at that time. I needed you to work with me the way we did without knowing so we could accomplish everything that we needed to and then I could tell you."

"Why?" Jonah asked. "Why couldn't you tell me at the beginning? I still would have worked with you. I still would have helped you with everything."

"But if you knew that I was Aubrey's father, you might have tried to get her involved or let her know what was happening and I couldn't let that happen. This is the way that it had to be. But I can explain it all now."

"Explain it to me, too."

Jonah turned around and saw Aubrey standing at the door to the bedroom. Her eyes were focused past him, locked on Frederick.

7

Mhavrych walked into the passenger section of the ship and glanced over at the one woman who was sitting there. She had purposely avoided being near any of the other passengers during the initial leg of the journey that had brought them from Earth to a small hub satellite where they dropped off everyone on the trip but her. But she didn't seem to notice. Her stance and behavior hadn't changed now that she was alone on the ship except for the pilot and the two flight attendants, including Mhavrych. He was still getting accustomed to traveling this way and found that he didn't much enjoy it. He hated the feeling of the ship moving beneath his feet and was frustrated by how slowly they transitioned from place to place. The portals and tunnels allowed him to shift from place to place and time to time in a matter of seconds. The ship took days to get from Earth to Uoria and he felt like they were wasting so much time as they slid through space. It made him feel anxious and out of control, but he had to force himself to stay focused and pay attention to the one human passenger who remained.

She had kept to herself since the moment that she got onto the ship, even ignoring his attempts and the attempts of the other flight attendant to interact with her and engage her in any sort of entertainment or even just conversation that might make the trip go by faster. It was obvious that she was a woman who stayed to herself and put a tremendous amount of emphasis on controlling and concealing her emotions. She seemed uninterested in making any sort of connections with anyone and only cared about what was right in front of her. She sat with her shoulders hunched over now, having tucked away the notebook that she had been scribbling in an hour before the last time he checked on her.

From what he had learned about her, this woman's name was Eliana and she was a journalist who was traveling to Uoria to write about the Denynso. Her knee bounced nervously, and her eyes occasionally darted back and forth as if she was waiting for something bad to happen. She sighed, pushing her hair back away from her face. I wondered what she was thinking about, what was making her so nervous. Even Eden hadn't seemed this uncomfortable and she knew that she was heading to the dangerous planet with a mission that was against the strict policies of her brutal hosts.

The pilot came back from the cockpit and smiled at her, still seemingly unfazed by her cold distance.

"It's about landing time Miss Eliana."

"Thanks," she replied keeping my eyes lowered away from him.

The pilot nodded and headed back into the cockpit. Mhavrych knew that he had already put the automatic landing sequence into action to ensure a smoother, more efficient placement of the ship when it arrived on Uoria, but the middle-aged human man preferred to be in the cockpit when the ship was on its way down just to make sure that he was close to the controls in case something happened. Eliana looked even more unhappy as the ship started to descend. She had chosen to forgo the passenger pods that provided a far more comfortable flight and landing experience, preferring the few seats that were like those on an airplane. Mhavrych knew that this was one of the last times that a ship like this would be used for such a long trip. There were too many problems, too many circumstances that could go wrong when traveling that far, and the newer technology provided for transits that were comfortable, safe, and easy to control.

Eliana gripped the sides of the seat and gritted her teeth, muttering under her breath as she seemed to brace herself for the impact of the ship. When the ship hit the ground softly and shuddered to a stop she let out the breath she had been holding and finally seemed to release some of the tension in her body. Looking as though she wanted to appear casual and unruffled, Eliana stood and immediately reached back, bracing her hand on the chair to regain her equilibrium.

She looked even more unsure now that they were on the ground, but Mhavrych didn't think it had anything to do with the trip itself. Now that they had arrived on Uoria she knew it was time for her to encounter the species that she had come this far to learn about. Though it was her intention all along and the entire reason she had come, Mhavrych knew that the reality that she was going to encounter a species that was known throughout the galaxy as the most ferocious warriors living must be unnerving.

The door to the ship slid open and Eliana visibly jumped. Her shoulders then relaxed slightly, as she let out a low chuckle. She shook her head and took a deep breath like she was trying to get herself under control. Gripping her bags tightly, she stepped out of the ship and into the dark of the planet beyond. The sky above was deep blue blended with brushstrokes of violet and sparkling with stars. Mhavrych followed behind her and watched as she filled her lungs with the clean, fresh air of Uoria. He could understand the compulsion. The air here was pure and sweet, filled with the scent of grass and rich dirt rather than the sometimes noxious, dense air that hung around the cities on Earth. That had been one of the most surprising elements of the planet the first time that he arrived. Mhavrych had immediately noticed that it was more difficult to breathe, that the air was thicker, heavier, and seemingly filled with other components that he had never experienced.

Mhavrych nearly called out to Eliana to warn her but had to remind himself that he wasn't to interfere to any extent beyond what was necessary or risk making changes that could be disastrous. Instead, he had to step back and watch as Eliana ran directly into the large man in front of her. Mhavrych immediately recognized him as Pyra, the head warrior who had been mated to Eden after she arrived. The strong orange eyes that stared down at Eliana when she looked up at him confirmed his status and her eyes widened in response to seeing him. Mhavrych wondered if this human woman had even seen a picture of a Denynso or knew anything about how they looked when she agreed to this assignment. It seemed something that she should have known prior to getting to Uoria if only to prepare herself, but she may have intentionally kept herself from knowing more about them, wanting to be able to record her most honest and thorough initial impression of them that she could.

"You're huge!" she exclaimed.

Pyra gave her a partial smile, apparently amused by her reaction to him.

"And you're tiny as can be, woman. You must be Eliana?"

The human woman didn't seem as amused by his reaction to her and Mhavrych noticed that she pulled herself up slightly as if trying to make herself look bigger even though she was miniscule when compared to him. From the human women that he had seen since going to Earth for the first time, it seemed to Mhavrych that she was rather small even for human women. She seemed very aware of this and bristled when she felt that anyone else might acknowledge it.

"Yeah, and you must be the famous Pyra."

There was an edge of stubbornness in her voice, like she was trying to prove to him that she wasn't intimidated by being flippant and dismissive.

"Famous?"

"Yep, you're a legend back home."

He shrugged, unfazed.

"Well, I guess that's a compliment then. The king and queen have been anxious about your arrival. You're doing a story about us? To make us more appealing to your kind?"

He seemed unimpressed by the idea of a human woman coming all the way to Uoria just to write about the Denynso. They were already incredibly well-known throughout the galaxy. They'd had no interaction with Earth in many years. To their knowledge, no humans had been on Uoria since then. Of course, Mhavrych knew this wasn't the case. He knew that the wreckage of the StarCity was lying across the planet and that the displaced Nyx 23 crew was locked in place within their settlement, awaiting release by the Denynso warriors and their human counterparts.

Mhavrych expected Eliana to continue to be defensive, but she surprised him by giggling.

"A series of stories, articles about what it's like here. Your King and Queen seem very determined to mix our species and helping each other out. It's a win-win really."

"Well let's go." Pyra reached out for her bags and took them so he could help her carry them toward the banquet hall where he would introduce her to Creia and Theia. "My mate has been complaining I'm not a gentleman. If only she could see me now."

"I'll be sure to tell her."

Eliana had a suspicious look on her face as she said it, as if she wasn't sure what she should think of the warrior being concerned about how his human mate felt about his behavior.

"Thanks, it's important that she knows I'm sweet right now. She's carrying my child."

Pyra started away from the ship and Eliana fell into step behind him. Mhavrych wanted to follow but didn't. He didn't want Pyra to see him and the place where the ship had landed ensured that the way to the banquet hall was exposed, giving him nowhere to hide as he trailed along behind them. The revelation of Eden's pregnancy was something that he hadn't expected. Though he knew that the scientist had a child in the future, he hadn't realized that she had become pregnant so soon after her arrival on Uoria. He wondered what that meant for her conversion into being a Denynso after the brutal attack from the Klimnu required her healing.

Mhavrych heard someone step out of the ship behind him and turned, expecting to see the other flight attendant coming out to stretch beyond the constraints of the ship for the first time in days. He had learned that he wasn't the only one who felt nearly smothered by the huge stretches of time they were contained within the ships when traveling between the planets. They were given a short reprieve after landing, but it wasn't nearly enough. When he turned, however, he saw the pilot coming toward him across the platform. He extended his hand toward Mhavrych, who looked at it for a few seconds before accepting it.

"Thank you for your service," the pilot said.

Mhavrych cocked his head at him.

"Excuse me?"

"I just received your special assignment orders. Congratulations."

Mhavrych was confused, but he nodded.

"Thank you."

"I must admit, I was surprised when I heard that you were to be immediately released from the rest of your contract so that you could participate in this assignment. I would have thought I would get more warning if something like that was going to come up."

He didn't sound angry, more like he was disappointed that he was having to give up one of his crew in the middle of a crossing. Mhavrych didn't know what was happening but continued to go along with it. He gave a slight shrug.

"I'm surprised, too," he said.

"Well, I wish you the best of luck and perhaps I will see you again so that you can tell me all about the assignment."

"I look forward to it."

"You are welcome to stay in the ship for the night, but I was told that a representative for the company would be arriving shortly to bring you to alternative accommodations so that you can be prepared for the early start tomorrow. If you prefer that, you can go gather your belongings from your quarters."

"Thank you," Mhavrych said again, still unsure of what else he could say. "I appreciate the opportunity you gave me."

In that moment he was being completely genuine, though he knew the pilot would never know just how much of an opportunity he did give him. Mhavrych's mind was racing, twisting and tangling as he desperately tried to figure out what might be happening and how he should be responding. Though there was a strong possibility that he could be walking into something dangerous, there was also a chance that one of the other members of the resistance efforts had traced him and come for him, though he didn't know how any would have done it. The risk was too high for him to ignore the call and to simply get back on the ship and continue back to Earth for the next stage of his mission. Instead, he would gather his belongings and face whoever might be waiting for him.

The single bag that contained the very few belongings he had with him as he traveled slung across his back, Mhavrych walked back through the ship and out again onto the platform. The night had gotten even deeper, the colors of the sky fading away into inky blackness that would deepen further before the sun began to rise again. He walked down from the platform into the dirt at the bottom of the steps and looked to either side, waiting for someone to approach. Several still, silent minutes passed before he noticed movement to the back of the ship. He felt his muscles tense and his stomach tighten as he prepared himself for whatever might happen. The figure came toward him and he noticed that it didn't look large. A few steps later it stepped into the light coming from the ship and he saw Kendra's lovely, serene face gazing at him.

"Good evening, Mhavrych," she said.

"How do you keep doing this?" he asked.

"How do you?"

"This is what I'm supposed to be doing. It's what my kind has always done."

She nodded slightly.

"This is what I'm supposed to be doing, too." She walked past him and started away from the ship across the open space in front of him. She had gone several steps before she paused and looked over her shoulder at him. "Aren't you coming?" she asked.

"Coming?"

She turned around and tilted her head at him, an amused smile on her lips.

"Didn't the pilot tell you that someone would be coming for you? For a special assignment?"

Realization hit him.

"You?" he asked. "You told him that I had been chosen for a special assignment and that you would be coming for me?"

She giggled.

"Did you want to stay with the ship longer?" she asked. "You could return to Earth with them if you'd like. Or you could follow me."

Follow me.

They were the words that she kept using, the instruction that she kept giving him. Mhavyrch knew it was what he needed to do. He tightened his grip on his bag and rushed after her, falling into step beside her just as Kendra started up again. He stared at her out of the corner of his eye as they walked along, but she barely seemed to notice that he was there. She walked along like she was floating, occasionally tilting her face up toward the sky to enjoy the soft touch of the breeze across her skin. They had been walking for several minutes when he finally turned to her.

"Where are we going?" he asked.

"I wonder how Eliana knew that Pyra was Eden's mate."

She said it as if she hadn't heard him at all.

"What?"

"Eliana knew that Pyra and Eden mated. Don't you think that's strange?"

"What do you mean?" Mhavrych asked. "Why would that be strange? She was coming to Uoria. Why wouldn't she know?"

"She's a journalist," Kendra said. "She's not a scientist. She's not in the University program. Why would she know? Do you think that's how Ryan found out about the baby, so he could try to kidnap him?"

She seemed to always speak in riddles, telling him things without telling him. Forcing him to figure things out for himself so that she didn't interfere. Perhaps she really didn't know the significance or what to do with the information. Perhaps she knew that only Mhavrych could resolve these things.

"How would that be, though?

She didn't answer as they continued walking. Mhavrych glanced at her again, realizing that there was something building inside of him. He found himself glad that she was there, happy to see her. It was an odd realization and one that he wouldn't have expected. He was usually utterly focused, completely consumed with the mission that he was on and all that he needed to do that the thought of being happy to see anyone in particular or even hoping that there would be someone there when he arrived at any specific place was far from his mind. When he first felt the glimmers of this type of feeling he was able to convince himself that he was only glad to see her because of his curiosity. He wanted to know who she was and what she meant in his life. He wanted to know how she had gotten her hands on the starstone she claimed he had given her, and what it meant that she was wearing it around her neck, refusing to give it to him until he came to retrieve it, even though she had seen him on several occasions now. Each time that he discovered her, it was another step, another piece of the puzzle.

But he could no longer tell himself that was it. Though he felt like he was getting closer, finding out more with every leap and every scene he witnessed, he also felt that he was becoming more and more drawn to Kendra. Something about her was intriguing and magnetic, unlike anything or anyone he had ever experienced. She drew him in and each time he saw her, he wanted to know more about her and experience more of her.

Suddenly she stopped and Mhavrych stumbled back a few steps to get back to her.

"What is it?" he asked.

"The pilot told you that a representative would be coming to bring you to alternate accommodations," she said, a hint of an amused smile on her face.

"I thought that was you," Mhavrych said.

Kendra shook her head. There was a slight rustle in the distance and Mhavrych turned toward it. He saw a figure with massive wings stretched to his sides lowering to the ground. His wings lowered to his sides and he took a few steps toward them.

"Hello, Kendra," the Eteri man said.

"Hello, Amoran."

"Is this him?"

She nodded and gestured toward Mhavrych.

"This is Mhavrych."

Amoran took a strap from the bag at his hip and

approached Mhavrych. Mhavrych took a step back and looked at Kendra.

"What's he doing?" he asked.

"Don't worry. He's just going to get you there faster. Unless you can fly, and I didn't know."

Mhavrych shook his head.

"No," he said.

"I didn't think so. Then you will need Amoran. He will get you in hours where it would have taken you days."

"I can travel through the tunnels."

"You could. But you would have to find one. And don't you want to see what others who travel the planet do?"

The way she said it was leading, suggestive just like nearly everything else she said. He didn't respond, but also didn't move away as Amoran approached. He got behind Mhavrych and used the strap to attach himself to Mhavrych's back. An instant later they left the ground and he could see Kendra rise up beside them. They flew slowly at first, but the higher they got, the faster they got until it seemed that everything around them was blurring. Mhavrych didn't like the feeling when they first rose into the sky, but the further they went, the more accustomed to it he became. He allowed himself to relax, trying to pay attention to what was around them even though he could see little of it. He tried to discern what Kendra wanted him to see or to experience, hoping that it might tell him something as they went.

He didn't know how long had passed since they took off, but he was relieved when he realized they were slowing and lowering back down toward the ground again. He waited while Amoran released the strap around them and then turned to Kendra, who landed delicately beside him.

"Where are we?" he asked.

"The Eteri kingdom," she said.

Mhavrych looked around.

"Why are we here?"

"So that you can rest," she said. "There's more to do."

She started walking toward the hills in the distance where Mhavrych could see doors built into the grassy sides. He followed her to one and ducked through the door to find himself in a small house decorated with furniture that appeared to be made from the vegetation that grew thick and lush at the edge of the village. Mhavrych noticed a series of objects sitting on a shelf on one wall and a wood carving sitting on a table to one side. Something about it looked familiar, but he couldn't place it. He looked over at Kendra as she took a step toward him.

"Welcome home."

8

"**Y**ou never said that this was going to happen."

Vyker turned toward Galadriel, feeling his heart squeeze painfully at the look of sadness and fear in his wife's eyes. She stood in the center of the room, seeming to avoid getting near their thrones or any of the doors, as though she was protecting herself by creating her own open space around her body. He had seen her do it before and though he didn't understand why she did it, he did what he could to respect her.

"I never said that what was going to happen?" he asked.

"You never said that he was going to be in danger like this."

"You knew what it meant when he became Protector, Galadriel. You knew it meant that it was going to be his responsibility to find the Key and to bring it safely back here."

"Yes," Galadriel said, her voice rising in intensity. "The Key. I knew that was his responsibility. I never thought that it meant he was going to get wrapped up in what Aegeus was doing or that he was going to be in as much danger as he is right now."

"We've been working with Aegeus for longer than he has," Vyker pointed out. "We've been assisting him and Martin since Mhavrych was a child. You can't expect that he wouldn't be a part of it when he got older."

"How can you be so dismissive about this?" Galadriel demanded. "How can you pretend like there's nothing happening, like it doesn't matter? Aren't you scared?"

"Of course, I'm scared," Vyker snapped. "Don't you think I spend every minute agonizing over what could happen to him when he's traveling? Don't you think that every day I'm waiting for someone to tell me he manipulated one of the streams wrong or that he interfered and caused something cataclysmic? He's my son, too, Galadriel."

"Then why do you seem like it doesn't bother you? You're acting like you don't think any of this is a problem."

"That's not how I'm acting," Vyker said. "I'm acting like there is nothing that I can do, because there isn't."

"But you're his father."

"I'm also the son of a man who did something extraordinary. I'm the son who went into the streams when I was never supposed to and tried to complete what my father started. I'm the son who thought that I had figured everything out and that I had made everything fine, only to realize later I was wrong. He's my child and I love him, but he's also a man. He's not doing anything that I didn't."

"It isn't your fault that you were wrong about the wall," Galadriel said. "Both of us thought that we had done everything that we needed to do. We thought that we had found all the stones and that was enough to seal the wall and keep the Universe safe. We didn't have any way of knowing about the Key or how important it was."

"Not knowing doesn't make it any better. All of existence is still at the same risk and Mhavrych is trying to fix that. We should have told him. I should be out there with him."

"No. You've done your duty. You put your life and everything else at risk to accomplish what you did. Now it's time for you to rule your people. The streams and portals are still protected for now. But if you leave again, it will only be a matter of time before the kingdom uncovers them and they all start traveling again. That's not what your father wanted and it's not what we want. It's too much. It's too dangerous."

"If I can't do it, we have to trust Mhavrych. He's found Rilex again. He will help him through."

"He won't speak to him," Galadriel said. "He holds so much anger. He feels betrayed by a man who he never met."

"He abandoned us," Vyker said, trying not to feel the pain and bitterness that always came through when he talked about his father's best friend. "He came back for such a short time, but then he left again. He could have stayed here. He could have returned home rather than going back to Earth. If he had done that, we would have found out about the Key sooner."

"You don't know that," Galadriel said. "He didn't even know about it. Your father died before he was able to tell him about it and he didn't write about it in his notes. Even if he had left Earth and come back here permanently, Rilex couldn't have helped you find out about the Key or supported Mhavrych through his early missions. You have to let go of that anger, Vyker. Both of you do. Remember how happy you were to see him when he first came back here with Jem and Angela. You forgave him then."

"I didn't know he was going to leave again."

"You have to let it go. He left because he knew that there was more that he needed to do."

"And yet you don't want your son to do what he knows that he needs to do."

"Because I don't understand why it has anything to do with Mhavrych. Why does it have to be him?"

"When Aegeus came here when Mhavrych was born, none of us knew anything about the Order. We didn't know about what was happening outside of our stream or about the Key. It's because of him that we learned about what my father did at the beginning of the war with the Travetori, the Valdicians."

"I refuse to call them that."

"But that's what they are," Vyker said. "When Valdin broke away from the rest, he created his own kind. They have been contorting and changing over the generations. Once they left this stream, they were no longer linked to their original kind. You know this as well as I do, Galadriel."

"No, Vyker. No, I don't know this as well as you do. This isn't my existence. This isn't my species. This isn't my history. I know you don't like to acknowledge that, but you have to. When you pretend that my past doesn't exist, it's like pretending I don't. You have to remember that I lived in a different time, in a different world, when I didn't know any of this had happened. I didn't grow up hearing the stories that you did. And you have never known what I did when I lived on Earth. That's why I can't understand why any of this has to do with Mhavrych. In my time, Uoria is still strong. Earth is still standing and there have been no invasions, no uprisings. Penthos is an empty planet that was the site of something horrific, but it was resolved. I don't understand why any of this is happening."

"That's what was happening when you were there," Vyker said. "It can change. It has changed."

"But what can any of that have to do with each other? On

Earth people haven't even heard of the Valdicians. I don't understand how Aegeus and Martin could have discovered Ryan's experiments. I don't understand why they are trying to stop him rather than protecting the Key. Mhavrych is crossing time and space so much, putting himself at more risk every time, and I don't understand how any of it could have anything to do with each other. Can't he just get the Key and bring it back as he was supposed to do all along? Wouldn't that solve everything?"

"No, Galadriel. It isn't that simple. Just like you said, this isn't your time. This isn't your stream. You came from a place where everything was as it was and there was no other option. You can't fathom how these intertwine because you are used to things simply being what they are without any flexibility. I had hoped that eventually you would be here long enough that you would get used to my world, but no matter how long you are here, I don't think that you will ever really understand."

Vyker could see the pain in his wife's eyes and wished that he had been more careful with the way that he had said it. In the timeline of her life, she had been in the stream with him for longer than she had been on Earth, yet she was still so controlled by the way that her life progressed when she was there. Her obsession with the segment of the temple, or the HM-1313 wall, as she knew it, had been their first connection to one another, but sometimes he had to remind himself that she was very firmly living on Earth. It wasn't until she reached out to a man she knew as Rick, who was actually Rilex, the best friend of Vyker's father, that their lives really crossed and the possibility of something beyond the structured, strict forward motion of her life became a reality.

"Do you wish that I never came?" she asked, her voice shadowy.

Vyker took several strides toward her, wanting to touch her, to reassure her.

"Never," he said. "I would never wish that. You are everything to me, Galadriel. I can't exist without you. I don't want to exist without you. But that doesn't change that I see things differently than you do. I can see why these things are all connected."

"Then tell me. Show me why. Make me understand why people scattered across the Universe, the streams, and time can be so linked that my son has been driven to what he's doing."

"When we met I told you about the StarKillers. I explained that they could rise up and destroy the Universe just as they had been destroying streams. That is the Valdicians. They were far stronger then than they are now, but they are getting stronger. I told you that we had to preserve the temple to save the Universe. That's when I thought that it was only sealing the wall and that it was only the knowledge inside that they wanted. Now we know about the Key my father hid with the Order, I can see what he was doing, and I can see the devastation that happened because he died before he was able to tell anybody what he had done. He never intended that. He wanted someone to know. He thought that the war would end, and he would be able to go retrieve the Key and restore the temple completely. The time that has passed since then has caused extensive damage to the edges of the streams."

"What do you mean?"

"They're collapsing in on themselves. The Universe is dying. Unless it can be pieced back together and the damage that has been done can be fixed, there might not be anything that can be done."

"How can this all be on his shoulders? How can this all be his responsibility?"

"When you were carrying Mhavrych, I told you that Orion was created for him. You said that constellation is still there, even during your time on Earth."

"It is, " Galadriel confirmed. "It is one of the brightest and most beautiful in the night sky."

"The only reason that can be is that our son made such an incredible impact on the Universe that he could never be forgotten. If you can still see that constellation, Mhavrych is still protecting the Universe. Remember what his name means, Galadriel. Remember what Aegeus told us the day that he was born."

Vyker could see her eyes soften, the tender mist of emotion falling over them as she envisioned, just as he had, the night that their first child, their son, came into the world. They had been anticipating him with such excitement, looking forward to every detail about being parents. They couldn't wait to hold him in their arms, to look into his face, to see what he looked like. This child had been critical to the completion of what they saw as their mission, the goal that had brought them together. They had found the star stones that they needed to fill the gaps around the temple wall, but there was one missing, one in the center of the wall that needed to be found. That was when they realized that they had had it all along. The stone that he had used to create the star to connect to Galadriel when she was on Earth was actually in celebration of their child, and it was that stone that they found to be a true star stone, the stone that was missing from the wall.

They had shared that story with Aegeus when he arrived

from Uoria, a stranger they weren't expecting from a species they didn't know. But he told them that he came on behalf of a secretive group created many years before, well before Vyker's birth, at the onset of the war with the darkened remnants of the species once known as the Travetori. Called the Order, these honored members of a species known as the Mikana had been chosen by Malan to be the guards and protectors of the Universe by holding the Key. They would hide this critical piece of the temple until Malan returned or the Chosen came to restore it. Their son's birth marked the birth of the Chosen and the future Protector. As Galadriel held him in her arms just moments after he came into the world, Aegeus came into the room and looked down at him, his expression as though he was looking beyond the newborn's face to the grandfather he had known decades before.

As he told the story of Malan risking his life, his kind, and everything he held precious in order to protect the Universe in the best way he knew how, Aegeus revealed a part of Vyker's father that was even more impressive and powerful than Vyker had ever known. This was so beyond the stones he had searched for. Malan had known that the stones were scattered and that the Valdicians were growing in number and in strength. Even if they were able to defeat those of them still on the Cassiopeian planet during the war, he knew there were more who had left, venturing into the portals to find the safety of the other streams. There they could nurture their strength and grow in their desire for dominance and control. It would take time to find the stones that would restore the temple. As long as the Key wasn't in the wall, though, he would never be able to gain the full power and strength of the knowledge in the temple.

Though this provided a new layer of protection,

ensuring that the Valdicians weakened over time, it also meant that the temple was incredibly unstable. Malan knew he needed to work quickly to find the stones. Once they were in place, he could return to the Order and reclaim the Key. When Malan died, the Order continued to carry on their duty to protect the Key. The two streams meant that the Order had already been for thousands of years by the time that Mhavrych was born and Aegeus brought the heavy news that things had changed. The Order was tainted by corruption. The Valdicians were growing stronger under new guidance. Though he didn't say it, Vyker knew that Aegeus was bringing him the news that the Universe was collapsing. A dark lord was rising and would bring the dissolution of all existence. This new child represented hope. The Chosen could find the Key that had long since been lost, its very existence reduced to a legend as the Order expanded and their missions broadened and changed. The situation had become so severe that Aegeus had stopped telling his beloved wife what was happening and was shielding his own children. They didn't know about the origins of the Order or of the Kintani. They didn't know about the Chosen who had just been born, and hopefully would never have to because all would be alright. In that moment he rested his hand on the baby's head and Vyker's son opened his eyes for the first time.

The shooting stars in his eyes were so bright they nearly washed out the rest of the color and his expression was so serene it was as though he had already lived a hundred lifetimes. Aegeus looked at him for a few seconds longer and then gave him his name. Mhavrych. Miracle.

9

Mhavrych clenched his fists, letting the pain of his fingernails digging into the heel of his hand keep him focused on staying absolutely still. He had to tell himself that what he was watching had already happened. It was a fixed moment, something that had to happen. As horrible as it was and as much as Mhavrych wanted to run forward into the throng and prevent the spilling of blood that was about to unfold in front of him, he couldn't. He had been warned, severely and intensely, about the destruction he could cause if he changed moments that led into others. There were things he could alter, moments he could manipulate, and there were those that were permanently etched in time. If he was to change them, he could stop the progress of time and trigger a ripple effect that could instantly result in Ryan coming into power and the Universe collapsing.

He had to show restraint. He had to do what went so severely against everything he knew and was comfortable with and be willing to follow. He still didn't understand, but he had to trust where Kendra guided him and that what she told him was what needed to be done.

Mhavrych pushed his fingernails harder into his hands as the figures began to appear in the field ahead of him. He stayed hidden in the shadows, watching intently even though he didn't want to, looking for what he was supposed to learn from this. The first group of warriors eased their way from out of the woods and made their way to the building that was hunkering in the distance. He knew that this was the building where Eliana had been kept prisoner by the Klimnu and where they had discovered a battered, broken, brutalized woman who barely survived the rescue. The Denynso wanted to destroy it, to wipe any sign of it from the planet, but what they didn't realize was that this building was a critical element of all that they would soon discover.

It was a prison. Mhavrych knew when it had been built and why, but the warriors were still focused entirely on the brutality that they had witnessed because of it and because of the tiny woman who had come to their compound and found love with the healer who saved Eden and then saved her.

The night sky split with balls of fire that shot out of the hands of some of the warriors and burst into bigger, more intense flames once they got inside. Smoke filled the air as the flames erupted, catching fire from all the dust and debris within the ancient building that had long been abandoned until the Klimnu decided to claim it as their own and use it to imprison and torture the women. This was what had led the Denynso down such a tangled path of confusion. They thought that the evil on Uoria and the danger that faced their kind and those they loved sat in the lap of the Klimnu. They hadn't yet discovered the Valdicians and the role that they played. The cloud of smoke filled the air and Mhavrych watched painfully as glass from windows covered with weathered bars and cages shattered into the air. Each sheet of glass exploded with a loud crack, punctuating the sizzling sound of the fire around and in the building. Mhavrych was transfixed by the raw, savage beauty of the fire and the bitter thought of the destruction as a cleansing that he almost didn't notice the appearance of the first grotesque Klimnu.

Searing red eyes scanned the warriors and a sense of heaviness settled over the area. Mhavrych moved slightly closer, relying on the warrior's focus to keep them from noticing that he was there, and found himself a few yards from Ciyrs and Eliana. They stood close together, but the sound of the fire was so loud they had to nearly shout to one another to be heard. This allowed their voices to travel to him through the smoke-laced air.

"I love you, now go get with the others. I need you to be safe."

Eliana wasn't moving. Mhavrych noticed that a change had come over her since she had been in the ship traveling here from Earth. Though she still seemed intense and was standing at a slight distance from the others, showing that she still wasn't entirely comfortable with people trying to engage with her. And yet somehow, she seemed softer, like her connection with Ciyrs had found something inside of her that needed to be both guarded and released, defended and exorcised.

"Go," Ciyrs insisted. "Ero and Ullie will take you to safety."

Mhavrych's ears pricked at the name "Ullie". He tried to remember the significance of it or even when he heard it. Nothing was coming to mind, but he knew that name meant something. That warrior had crossed his path before now, but he couldn't remember.

"I—I don't know if I can leave you," Eliana said.

She was suddenly gone from his side and the battlefield swarmed with Klimnu. The Denynso rushed forward, their inborn desire for war pumping through their blood, fueling them as they clashed with the pale, slimy creatures in the intense glow of the fire. Mhavrych watched as one of the Klimnu snuck up behind Ciyrs. It made a sound that made Mhavrych's skin crawl and dragged his claw down Ciyrs's cheek, immediately drawing blood.

"Why would they let you stay around? You're nothing but the useless healer."

The words were barely audible, but Mhavrych could see the healer's face darken. He wasn't a warrior. He wasn't born to train and to fight, and yet he was there on the field with those who had been bred for this, who had been trained and cultivated from the time they were old enough to follow the instructions. In Mhavrych's eyes, that made him even more intimidating. He might have been born for something else within his clan, created for the purpose of healing those who were injured or ill, and was never given the skills of the warriors, but he was strong and courageous enough to walk into war and face down the brutality of the unknown.

In a movement so fast, it seemed that he barely even controlled it, Ciyrs reached forward and wrapped his hand around the neck of the Klimnu. In an instant, the creature let out a scream that cut into Mhavrych's core and burst into flame. The scent of burning flesh filled the air and the creature was rapidly reduced to nothing more than a pile of ash.

Mhavrych saw the startled look on the healer's face and knew that the death of the Klimnu had been something he hadn't expected, that had shocked him as much as it did

Mhavrych. Ciyrs didn't have time to dwell on the newfound ability, however. There was more fighting erupting around him, getting more and more vicious as the moments passed and the ground was splashed with blood. It was as if the hotter the fire burned and the more destruction it caused, the harder and more intensely they fought, wanting it all to come to an end.

Suddenly Ciyrs noticed one of the creatures jump onto Creia's back and ran toward him, determined to rescue his king. He reached out and touched the creature, instantly causing the beast to erupt into flames. This Klimnu survived longer than the other, pulling itself away from the healer's touch and screaming as it ran around the battlefield as if trying to escape the pain that it was obviously suffering. It was only seconds later, though, it stopped, and its body disintegrated into ash that was picked up by the wind and carried away.

Mhavrych looked beyond the battle to the building, trying to understand all that had happened in that one place. He knew that the Klimnu had been a source of incredible hatred for the Denynso for some time and that the two species often fought, resulting in extensive bloodshed and loss of life. But the prison had been there for so long, forgotten, and totally unknown to the Denynso. And suddenly the Klimnu had decided to use it, to take over and fill it with their own prisoners as if emulating the prison that thrived on Penthos for years. The thought suddenly occurred to him that three of the women now living among the Denynso were nearly killed by the Klimnu, each overtaken by the creatures when they were vulnerable. Though Eden had never ended up in the prison, she could have. A disguised Klimnu, one with a unique and extraordinary ability, had made it so that she thought she was coming out of the house to talk with her mate.

Something about that stuck with Mhavrych. It held onto him, but he wasn't sure why. He continued to watch the vicious battle until the Klimnu retreated, then rushed away, not wanting to be seen.

Something else happened in that prison. They didn't imprison the women just because they wanted to. There was something else. Something more. Mhavrych knew that he had to delve deeper.

"Fifty-five days."

This was the hardest that Mhavrych had fought to control himself since he started manipulating the streams and moving through time as he needed to. He stood in the prison, knowing what was coming, knowing that in a matter of days the building where he was now would be engulfed in flames from the hands of the Denynso. For now, though, it was heavy with the scent of blood and death and reverberating with screams. The woman in the cell in front of him looked as though she had been emptied out of herself and her body tattered. She was a shell, bruised and streaked with blood, her eyes sunken, her hair matted. Everything inside Mhavrych said to rush the Klimnu that was standing there beside her and destroy him so that he could set this fragile woman free, but he couldn't. The days had to progress as they had. They had to unfold exactly the way that they had or the purpose of the prison within the puzzle that they were solving would never be uncovered.

There was another shattering scream and the woman

looked around, obviously terrified. The Klimnu standing near her laughed.

"You hear our new guest," he said. "She is different than you. She is special."

"What do you mean?"

It sounded painful just for the words to come out of the woman's mouth. From where he stood in the dark shadows of the cell across from the woman, Mhavrych could see that her lips cracked when she spoke, and his skin shivered slightly. It was something so small, so seemingly inconsequential, and yet it somehow took the brutality of what she was going through to another level.

"The Denynso will come for her." The Klimnu said. "She belongs to one of them and he will ensure they find her, which means he will bring the warriors right to us."

Mhavrych knew that he was talking about Eliana. She was the one who was being tortured as she was used as bait. He had learned that the Denynso were able to communicate with their mates through their thoughts and the sickening realization rolled through him that the creatures were putting her through as much fear and agony as they could in an effort to reach out to Ciyrs. They wanted to lure him to her because they knew that if he came, the warriors would come along with him. The battle they were hungry for would be handed right to them. The fight hadn't been an accident or an unexpected ambush. It had been orchestrated.

The rest of the night was cold and horrific. Mhavrych stayed exactly where he was, shivering in the damp cold, his joints and muscles aching from sitting on the stone floor. He was trying to find a position that was even close to comfortable, but then he thought of the woman across the corridor form him. She didn't even know he was there. She had no concept that he was crouched on the floor, trying to keep himself warm, trying to ignore the smells and the sounds. He knew that he could have left, but in the same way, he knew he couldn't. He had the compulsion to be there for this woman. Even if she didn't know that he was there, he wanted to be there until she got out. He wished that she didn't have to feel so alone.

The next morning, the moment finally came. Barely more than bones from the nearly two months that she had spent in the prison, the woman was able to slip through the bars of her cell and get into the hallways to search for help. Mhavrych so desperately wanted to help her, but he knew this wasn't his place. Eliana had to find her. She had to rescue her.

Mhavrych waited until the woman got fully out of her cell and made it down the hallway before getting out of the cell where he had spent the night and starting down the hallway in the opposite direction. Something shimmered in the distance and he noticed a pink light move around the corner at the end of the corridor. He rushed to catch up to it and saw Kendra strolling casually down another hallway, moving deeper into the building.

"Kendra, why did I have to watch that?" he asked.

"Watch what?"

"Any of it," he said. "Why did I have to watch that battle or the girl trying to escape?"

"She did escape," Kendra said. "Her name is Leia. She is one of the women from Earth."

"I gathered that," Mhavrych said. "But I don't understand why I needed to see any of that."

"You'll understand soon enough," Kendra said. "Think about it."

"Tell me."

She shook her head.

"I can't," she said. "I can't tell you. You have to find out for yourself. You have to follow the trail."

"I thought that I was following you."

"I am the trail," she said. "Think about what you've seen. Think about what you saw happen in that battle and what you realized about the prison. Then think about a question that you asked me. You need to keep going. There's more that you need to see."

"I don't want to see any more. I hate having to just stand there and not be able to help. I have to watch these horrible things happen and there's nothing that I can do to change them."

"That's right," she said. "There is nothing that you can do to change them. Those moments have happened, and they secured themselves in time. They are anchors. The extent of the ripples would not be worth the satisfaction of dropping a pebble through the surface of the water. But you can prevent them from happening again. You can prevent the devastation that Ryan has planned. He doesn't even know what he could do, Mhavrych. He wants power and absolute control, but he is more volatile and unpredictable than even he knows. He doesn't understand that by seeking out power and wanting to claim and hold providence over the Universe, he is actually damning it. But that doesn't have to be. The future can continue and the world can be preserved. But in order to do that, you have to see the moments that will support that future. You need to understand the events that cradle the possibility of that future within them. You have to try to be strong, Mhavrych. You have to see beyond what you can't change, no matter how terrible it seems. When you witness a birth, you have to see the beauty of the new life, not the blood on the midwife's hands."

Mhavrych immediately thought of Dove and the privilege of seeing her in the earliest moments of her life. He remembered nothing but how sweet she looked and the impact of realizing that she was now a queen and the mother of a species. He had to carry on. He had to ensure that she had a future to rule in and a planet to rule on.

MHAVRYCH WALKED UP and down the tunnel several times, noting each time that he felt himself pushed through the loop that connected him from one spot to one a far distance away across the planet. He knew that feeling. It was completely familiar to him and had become something that he usually barely noticed. Now, though, it hit him strongly as he made his way along the narrow path. He barely fit in it, confirming what the Denynso warriors had suspected when they stopped outside the entrance and said that they wouldn't fit through. Mhavrych had waited until the group left after their first visit through the tunnel to go in and explore it himself. It startled him when he realized that he was traveling not just along a tunnel that led down into an underground area of the planet, but through the delicate unseen barrier between each place and time. He moved through it several times to ensure that was what he was experiencing. As he did, he realized there was something strange about it. This wasn't just him moving through like he naturally did. Instead, it felt harsher, like it had been forced.

Not knowing how to interpret that feeling or what it might mean, Mhavrych finally continued down the tunnel. When he reached the end, he saw what looked like a small world open in front of him. It was difficult to interpret at first, looking like a wide pond bordered on one side by formations of rocks and on the other by trees. The longer that he looked at it, however, the more details that Mhavrych began to notice and soon he realized that he was looking at not water stretched across the ground, but a reflection of the sky, and the trees that he saw were upside down, their leaf-covered branches stretching out across the expanse as their roots crept across the stone overhead. A realization struck Mhavrych.

This is what he had heard about from his parents when he was a child and they told him the story of preserving the wall. They had described this place to him and told him of the important event that had happened here.

It was only days later that Mhavrych, crouching in the darkness of a formation of boulders where no one had seen him, witnessed it unfold. Even if he had stood up in that moment, he didn't think that anyone would have noticed him. The space was filled with the sound of battle, the air thick and tense with the fury of the fighting that was happening just feet away but that Mhavrych couldn't participate in, even though he so desperately wished that he could. The Klimnu swarmed the cavern, the disgusting creatures lashing out against the mix of Denynso and humans who had come together to fight. Men and women had become warriors, putting all of themselves into the cause that was bearing down on them, even as Mhavrych knew that they were still standing just at the precipice of all that would soon crack open in front of them.

Suddenly Eliana, looking stronger and braver now after spending more time in the compound with her Denynso mate and discovering her abilities as a healer, surged forward into the fray. Mhavrych watched her run toward one of the Klimnu that was climbing up the side of a tree toward where Pyra was positioned. Without hesitation, she reached out and grabbed it by its neck. The grisly pale creature screamed, the sound reverberating through the space and piercing through the rest of the sounds of the fight. Just as the creatures had under Ciyrs's touch during the battle outside of the prison, the Klimnu burned and dissolved away into ash as Eliana touched it. The smell tinged the air and Mhavrych recoiled slightly, as disgusted by the image now as he was then. Another of the human women, the young one named Samira who had come to Uoria after Ero broke all tradition of the Denynso and left the compound so that he could travel to Earth and reclaim his mate Zuri, burst out of the tunnel. She had been hiding there throughout the battle, seeming too afraid to be a part of it.

Now, though, she seemed compelled to involve herself, to do her part to defend those she had come to love. Her mate, Ty, was there among the other Denynso warriors who were battling against the Klimnu. Mhavrych had been watching him, fascinated by his presence among the others. On first glance, he looked just like the other Denynso men. He had the towering, imposing height, and massive, chiseled body. His skin was the same vibrant shade of blue, his eyes the bright orange that indicated his eternal link and unbreakable connection to his mate. But there was something about him. Something just slightly different enough that it made him stand out against the rest of them. Mhavrych wondered if anyone else noticed when they first looked at him or if it was something that was obvious only because he already knew. When he looked into Ty's face he saw the hint of something that he had seen since he was a child, but only in pictures, only in the shared memories of his parents.

He saw the Valdicians.

The reality was that this man was the descendant of the powerful, evil creatures that were the focus of his work, the purpose of all that he was doing. It wasn't a close link. Ty himself hadn't even known about his heritage until Creia had revealed it just recently. This man was the product of the mysterious and fabled link between the Valdicians and the Denynso that Lucian had mentioned. Few knew that when Aida and Fayat left Uoria, sent away by the Order in order to protect them, that Aida was carrying a child. This child was the very first of the hybrids that would inspire the future experiments of Ryan's ancestors, though they were never able to get their hands on him. The Order was still pure then. They hadn't yet fallen to the corruption. They hadn't yet been uncovered for their source of incredible power or their influence. They were still the most trusted and revered allies of Malan, Mhavrych's grandfather, Vyker's father. When the elder of the Order at that time saw Fayat and heard of his defection from the Valdician forces that had invaded and met the Eteri and the Denynso in battle, they knew the danger that he was in. They above all on Uoria knew the Valdicians and what they represented. Fayat didn't know about the Key. Mhavrych didn't know if any of them did. All they knew was the commands of their leader, Boaz, the direct line of Valdin. All they knew was their drive to claim the Universe for their control.

It was many years before the family of Fayat and Aida returned to Uoria to rejoin her clan. The generations that followed sank into the Denynso until they couldn't be differentiated, never showing any of the indications that anything flowed through their veins but the blood of the warriors. It wasn't until Ty's father was born that anything seemed different. Then Ty came, getting older and demonstrating a powerful gift that was unlike any of the warriors. His ability to move things with his mind was astonishing to those who knew nothing of his heritage, but to Creia it was the suggestion of a beginning. It was a reminder of all that had happened on the planet and everything the inhabitants had been through. Mhavrych knew, however, that even the King didn't know everything that had occurred so many generations before. Though he knew that the Denynso Kings were each individually a trusted ally of the Order in their time until Aida and Fayat left, Creia didn't know the origin of the group or why it was so important. He knew only that it was ancient and critically important. He couldn't approach them when he began to notice Ty's ability. The link between the species had been broken so long before and he had never intended to leave the compound.

Even if Creia had been able to go to the Order to tell them what he knew about Ty, however, Mhavrych doubted that he would have recognized the importance. As far as the Denynso King and nearly all others on Uoria knew, the Valdicians had left generations before and had not had any interaction with the planet since. They didn't know of how much they had actually done in the time that had passed since they first fought in the Badlands. To Creia and the rest of the Denynso, the most pressing danger that they were facing was the Klimnu. They believe that the grotesque creatures were their greatest threat and the enemy that could take over the planet if permitted. They had no way of knowing that it was the Valdicians that had orchestrated that threat. It was the Valdicians that had ensured the Klimnu would come into being and would continue the campaign of destruction and violence against the Denynso that the Valdicians had intended since so long ago.

It was knowing, that made it even harder for Mhavrych to watch as Samira ran toward her mate, only to have one of the Klimnu drop down from the tree to land in front of her, bringing a scream from her lips. The creature approached her, his eyes rolling as he clicked his claws together and ran his disgusting tongue across his lips. It reached for her and she screamed again. Instantly, Ty knew that she was in trouble.

"Samira!" he shouted.

"Ty," Samira screamed. "Get me."

Samira suddenly lifted into the air and Mhavrych knew that Ty had picked her up with his mind, utilizing the power that he had had since birth to rescue his mate. It was a strangely, bitterly ironic moment as she rose high above the Klimnu and was able to kick the creature directly in the face. The force of the impact sent the Klimnu tumbling backward so that he fell into the expanse of sky that stretched between the trees and the rocks. The skin-crawling sound that came from its mouth faded as it fell and disappeared, reminding Mhavrych of the mysterious depth of what had looked like water. He turned his attention back to Samira and watched as she got to Ty, who instructed her to take hold of a vine a few feet below where he clung to the tree. He pointed to a branch that would offer her a more stable resting place.

"Jump onto that branch. Keep holding onto the vine for stability, and just swing onto it. Stay there."

She followed his instructions without hesitation, closing her eyes and wrapping her hands tightly around the vine before she jumped. Mhavrych felt a pang of concern and then she hit the branch. Samira worked quickly to tangle a vine around her legs, using it to lash her to the branch so that she couldn't fall or be knocked off. The sound of the fighting and the nauseating smells of the battle were getting more intense, but the Denynso and those helping them seemed unaffected by it. Klimnu rose up into the air and were easily tossed away under the unseen force of Ty's mind. It didn't escape Mhavrych how odd it was that these Klimnu were totally oblivious to their own origins. By this point in their timeline, they had adopted their own stories of how their species had developed and why. They had their own understandings of why they had come to be. There was no knowledge that they had anything to do with the Valdicians and the hatred between the two species had already begun. Though only the most corrupt on Uoria knew, Ryan had long wanted one of the grisly but undeniably powerful creatures to include in his experiments and had chosen instead to create his own by capturing the Mikana man who had been fighting against the creation of the hybrid army for decades, Aegeus.

But Ty wasn't the only one of the Denynso warriors who used the unique features given to him by his unique heritage to fight. As Ty used his mind to lift the Klimnu and toss them out of the way, the youngest and smallest of the warriors, Ero, use incredible speed to run around the space, preventing himself from being caught or even from falling into the open sky by moving from surface to surface without pausing. This was a gift from a bloodline that he, too, had been unaware of until Creia told him about him at the same time that he told Ty of his Valdician heritage. That was another moment that Mhavrych had witnessed, watching as the faces of the young warriors changed as they registered what their King was telling them. Both thought that they were nothing more than Denynso. It had hit them hard to learn that they carried the blood other species. For Ty, the thought that he was much like the father he had lost when he was very young was a source of excitement and while he had been surprised and upset to learn about this unknown part of himself, there was also an element of relief knowing why he was so different. For Ero, though, the news would carry even more meaning.

When the young, beautiful warrior had learned that there was something more in him he was forced to face that he was part Mikana, which meant that running through him was the potential for the same horrible fate as these Klimnu. But they didn't know that yet. They didn't know of the Mikana or of their link to the Klimnu. For now, they knew nothing. For now, they were just Denynso warriors in the claws of battle, fighting to eliminate the species that had tortured them for so long.

"Jem, no!"

The tormented scream that came from Ty brought Mhavrych's attention away from the bloody scene of Pyra tearing one of the creatures apart with his bare hands, seeming to relish the feeling of the skin ripping and the bones coming apart. All those near Ty turned in the direction that he was looking and Mhavrych followed their gaze. There were few of the Klimnu left and the warriors would soon be victorious. With a sinking feeling in his stomach, Mhavrych knew that meant he had come to the moment that he had dreaded. He was about to watch something indescribably horrific, something that would change the course of existence in ways that were purely unimaginable for all of them. He didn't want to see it. And yet it was a critical turning point that he had heard about his entire life and he felt strangely privileged to witness it even if not stepping in, not saving the Denynso clan the agony they would soon face made his chest ache.

He turned his eyes toward the warrior who stood on one of the branches, far out across the sky. Jem was locked in a vicious hand to hand clash with one of the few remaining

Klimnu and two more had recognized his vulnerability and abandoned what they were doing, creeping toward him. It was clear that they knew they were beaten. There was no denying that the warriors and those who had stepped up beside them in battle had destroyed them and now the remaining creatures were focused only on their desire for as much devastation as they could manage. Each was driven for the satisfaction of taking a Denynso life. Jem was unafraid. He looked at each of the creatures fully and without hesitation. There was nothing in his stance that showed he was concerned or that he was going to try to escape from them. He punched one of the Klimnu with enough force to knock the thin, slimy being off balance, and the creature reached out to grab Jem by his shirt. Mhavrych looked over at Ty. Though he knew what was going to happen, the inevitable outcome, he still felt anxiety tightening in his chest and closing his throat. What was going to happen had to happen, but he still didn't want it to happen. Part of him was clamoring for one of the other warriors to run to Jem's aid or for Ty to be successful in his efforts to pick the other warrior up and pull him away from the danger.

Ty was concentrating hard on his goal and he managed to lift Jem a few feet off the branch, but the Klimnu that had a grip on him tugged him back down. Pyra dropped the last of the Klimnu body he held and ran toward them but stopped with Jem held up one hand to stop his leader.

"Stop, Pyra. Don't come out here. You're what they want. Remember, they are trying to get to Creia. If they kill our leader, they weaken our defenses and they can get to the king. There's only one way to stop them, and that is to eliminate them."

Jem's voice was steady and determined. It expressed no

fear and no questions. He knew exactly what he was saying, and he was willing to face what he seemed to know was going to happen. He fought against the control of Ty's mind, encouraging the Klimnu to pull him down even harder.

"Let me pick you up!" Ty screamed, desperate to save his friend from the horror that was waiting for him.

The pain in his voice was obvious, making what Mhavrych was watching even more difficult to stomach.

"No! Put me down," Jem shouted. "I'll be fine. These are the last of their kind here and there is something about me that they don't know."

One of the Klimnu gave a mirthless laugh at Jem's declaration and dragged his claws down the warrior's face, leaving a trail of blood against his skin.

"And what is that?" the creature asked, his voice almost lilting in its tone as he mocked Jem, clearly unimpressed.

Jem smiled and Mhavrych could see the calm, confident serenity on his face. There wasn't even a moment of hesitation in his mind. He had already given himself over to what he was going to do.

"I've always wanted to fly."

Jem reached out and wrapped his arms around the three creatures that had approached him. With a final glance up at his fellow warriors, he let himself fall backward from the branch and into the sky. Ty screamed and began to fight against the vines that were looped around his body, trying to get down to the branch. There was nothing that he could do, but Mhavrych knew that wasn't in his mind. All the warrior cared about was trying to get to Jem, trying to save him.

"Stop, Ty," Samira demanded, grabbing him and pulling him back toward her.

He looked at her with desperation etched on his face and Mhavrych could see her struggling to control her own emotions as she focused outside of herself and on her mate, wanting to comfort him even through her own pain.

"I let him die! He was right there."

She held him tighter. The tears sparkled in her eyes, but she forced herself to give the hint of a smile as she continued to stare at him.

"Stop. He did what he wanted to do. It's alright. He's among the stars now."

Mhavrych sank back further into the rock formation. Even though he had been out of sight during the fighting, he had been drawn out of his original place and now felt exposed, almost as though they could glance up and notice him at any moment. Now that the furor of the battle was over, they didn't have the chaos to distract them and he couldn't risk being seen, especially in the emotional turmoil of Jem's sudden disappearance. Mhavrych knew in their minds that when they watched him, they felt in their hearts that they had just witnessed his death. He knew that wasn't the case. He knew that Jem hadn't died but had arrived on the distant planet that thrust him into the world of his parents. To those who loved him, what Jem had just done was an end. To Mhavrych, it was a beginning. It was because of that sacrifice that the Universe had a chance to be saved.

Ahead of him, Mhavrych noticed movement and he sank back even further, pushing himself as far into the crevice as he could so that he felt the rocks pressing into his skin and could no longer see any of the warriors or the humans with them. He could hear them. The tears were audible in their voices and in the way they gasped for breath. But he sensed they were now moving out of the realm, needing to return to the Denynso compound above to at once share the news of their victory and their loss.

He watched as a woman came into view ahead of him.

She glanced slightly to the side, as if for a moment she could see him, but she said nothing. There was a faint glow around her and Mhavrych was immediately reminded of the pink light that surrounded Kendra, but this woman didn't look like her. She had no wings and her hair hung thick and silver down her back. This was an Irisa woman, one of the kind that despite their peaceful nature had come to be known as the Silver Warriors. He thought of what Aegeus and Casimir had told him. He remembered that when Aegeus walked out onto the battlefield to face the corrupt members of the Order that he was flanked by Irisa men, two of the rare members of the species who engaged in warfare. It was because of them that he was able to leave the field under the disguise of a reflection of the landscape around him. The plan had been to meet with Casimir in the war room and return to the battlefield to decimate the corrupt members of the Order and the rest of the Klimnu. It had never happened.

Mhavrych watched this Irisa woman for a few moments before he realized that it must be Loralia. She was alone in the realm, the last of her kind now. As he thought of this, Mhavrych noticed a hint of pink shimmer appear behind Loralia and then disappear. He crept through the rocks to follow it, knowing that it was Kendra. Once away from the chamber he found himself roaming through the silent, empty village that had once been the home of the Irisa. The feeling of them, the presence of the beautiful and talented species that had been wiped out so suddenly and so mysteriously, leaving behind only the one tiny woman who was now trying to understand why she had been left and how she was going to move forward on her own.

"Have you figured it out?"

Kendra walked out from one of the buildings and tilted her head at Mhavrych in the way that she so often did.

"That was someone's home," he said.

Kendra glanced over her shoulder at the building that she had emerged from and then nodded at him.

"I know," she said. "It's lovely inside."

"Because it's the way that it was left."

He felt protective of the emptied village, almost as though he needed to guard it as a shrine to those who had been lost. He didn't understand the compulsion. He had never had any strong personal link to the Irisa, and in his time as Protector, he had encountered countless abandoned homes, emptied villages, and decimated creatures. This place, though, felt somehow different.

"Have you figured it out yet?"

She had returned to her original question and Mhavrych narrowed his eyes at her.

"Another riddle."

"Not a riddle. Just a question."

She started to walk away from him and as he always did, Mhavrych fell into step behind her. In this moment it wasn't as much about going where she wanted him to as it was about not being caught by Loralia if she returned to the village. He didn't know how she would respond to seeing them there and the rippling changes that it could cause.

They walked until they reached another set of tunnels. He waited to feel the shift that would tell him that this section brought him through another of the unusual portals, but he never felt it. Instead, they walked directly out of the tunnels and into the lush woods that he recognized as the Eteri kingdom. Without him even realizing it, she had just told him something else. It was another piece, another detail that he would have to tuck away until it's meaning became more apparent.

"What are you talking about?" he asked. "Have I figured what out?"

"The village is empty," she said. "They're all gone."

"Yes," he said. "They were all killed in the Plague."

"Except for Loralia."

Mhavrych nodded, remembering what he had been told about the woman.

"Because of her father. Azrael. He's Eteri. That protected her."

"Doesn't it seem strange that the first time the Plague happened, the Irisa found sanctuary in the village?"

"Why is that strange?"

"They went below ground so that they could get away from what was making them so sick. And it worked. They stopped dying off and were strong and happy here. But the second time the Plague came, they were destroyed. It happened twice. The two times that Uoria was invaded."

Realization settled over Mhavrych.

"By the Valdicians."

Kendra nodded.

"Do you understand now?"

Mhavrych thought about what she had said, and a question formed in his mind.

"Why weren't they safe the second time?"

"Think, Mhavrych. Think about what you've seen. It's almost time. It's almost time for you to find me. Then you can come for me and for the stone."

Mhavrych felt a surge of emotion within him. Not fully understanding the compulsion, he took the few steps to close the space between Kendra and himself and wrapped his arm around her waist. His mouth met hers and he kissed her deeply. She returned the kiss, melting into him for a few moments before pushing away from him.

"What's wrong?" Mhavrych asked.

"You have to find me," she said. "It's all happening so quickly. You must go back to Aegeus and Casimir soon. There so much left to be done."

For the first time, there was something close to fear in her voice and Mhavrych knew that he had to keep going. His feelings for her had grown but she was still at a distance from him. He needed to follow through, discover the pieces, and ensure that it all came together before everything, including Kendra, was lost.

10

"Aubrey."

Frederick took a few steps toward her, but Aubrey took a step back, holding up her hand to stop him from getting any closer. She shook her head slightly. Tears were burning at the backs of her eyes, but she was refusing to let them run down her cheeks. She didn't know what emotion was inspiring those tears and she didn't want to give him the satisfaction of seeing them and being able to give them whatever meaning he wanted to. Until she was able to sift through everything that she was feeling and understand what it meant for all that was happening, she wasn't going to give herself permission to express it or anyone else permission to interpret it.

"I need you to tell me what's going on."

"I haven't seen you in so long," he said.

She nodded.

"Exactly. Years. It's been years. I haven't seen you since you and Mom left for yet another of your business trips and just haven't come back yet." She felt the color drain from her face. "Where is Mom?"

Frederick shook his head, understanding exactly what she was feeling.

"She's fine," he reassured her. "She just couldn't come with me this time."

"Of course, she couldn't," Aubrey scoffed angrily.

"Don't be like that," Frederick said.

"Why?" Aubrey asked. "Because I'm an adult? Because I'm fully grown now so I shouldn't be hurt that my parents don't want anything to do with me? Parents who supposedly wanted a child more than anything in the entire world, but then once you got me decided that you just couldn't hand it and didn't want to be parents anymore?"

"Why would you say that? Who told you that?"

"It was pretty obvious," Aubrey said. "But Nana told me when we talked about it. She said that the two of you just weren't able to reconcile the life that you had built for yourselves when you thought that you were never going to be able to have a child with the one that you got when you actually ended up with one. She said that you loved me, but that you needed to be able to keep doing the things that you were already doing."

"She never should have told you that," Frederick said.

"Why? Is it not the truth?"

"Your mother and I love you more than we could ever tell you. You are everything that we ever wished for."

"No, I'm not. You wanted your own child."

"You are our child. I don't care how you came to be my daughter, but you are my daughter and I love you just as much as if it was the two of us who conceived you and your mother who carried you. There is no difference. And it's because we love you so much that we worked even harder. We didn't want to think that our child lived in a world that wasn't safe. We couldn't bear the thought that you wouldn't grow up or that when you did you wouldn't be able to have the life that you deserve."

"What do you mean by that?" she asked.

Jonah stepped forward.

"Frederick has been working with a crew that uncovered the experiments that Ryan's family started. The operation is much bigger than any of us thought and could be far more dangerous. He has been working with them and the faction on Uoria to bring him down. But it's more than that. It's so much more."

Aubrey felt like another wave of shock had just rushed over her. She had never known what her parents did or why they were always gone. She had always just been told that they were working, that they had to be away, and she had never thought to question it when she was a young child. As she got older, she wondered more, but by then she had already started to accept the reality that she was never going to have the close-knit relationship with her parents that she saw in others and that her true home, her true happiness, was going to come with Nana.

"What do you mean?" she asked.

"What's happening here on Earth is only one part of something so much bigger."

"I know that," Aubrey said. "Jonah is from the Nyx 23 project. He landed on Uoria. I know about that planet and about Ryan and his experiments."

"And about the Valdicians?"

"Ryan's minions? Of course."

"They aren't his minions," Jonah said.

"I know that he's a descendant of one and that he intends to be the ruler when they rise into power, but they do everything he says and ensure that he never has to be involved in of the actual dirty work that he wants done."

"They are much more powerful than that," Frederick said. "That's what you don't understand. That's what none of us understood. From the very beginning, it's been the Valdicians. All of this started with them. They caused all of this to happen and they could have caused so much more destruction, but something weakened them. It couldn't destroy them, but it weakened them to the point that they weren't able to complete what they had set out to do. Then the experiments began. The goal shifted from using their own strength and capabilities to take over to using their bred super army of hybrids to take over. Once each of the planets fell to them, the army could be eliminated without concern because they were nothing more than commodities. That would leave only the pure-bred Valdicians and Ryan. He wanted to be the only hybrid left so that he was all-powerful, even more so than the rest of his species."

"I don't understand what any of this has to do with you," Aubrey said. "What could any of that have to do with you adopting me and then barely being around? Or never telling me that you were involved in something like this?"

"And never telling me who you were," Jonah added. "In all the time that we've been together, you never mentioned that you were her father. You knew that she is my wife, yet you only said that you knew Nana, not that you were her son."

"I already told you," Frederick said. "It was too much for you to take right then. I didn't want you to be thinking about Aubrey and all that this meant for her. You needed to be thinking about the mission that was at hand. After that was complete, I intended to tell you."

"What happened?"

"Things didn't go as easily as I hoped. We ran out of time and had to get back to the factory before I was ready. There was more that I had wanted to do, but I couldn't figure it out in time and I had to get back to make sure that Jonah was there to save you. I never got the chance to tell him who I was."

"I still don't understand," Aubrey said. "You keep saying that you were away for so long and that you did so much, but I was talking to Jonah in the basement of the factory just a few minutes before he pulled me out of the hallway. How is it possible that you could have done anything? And why did he change so much?"

"How is it possible that he's here at all when he boarded a ship to go to Uoria more than 115 years ago?"

"That's different," Aubrey argued.

"Is it?"

She didn't know what to say. She was confused, and her head was spinning. She hated feeling so out of control. She hated feeling like she didn't understand anything that was happening around her and that there was nothing that she could do to change it.

"Yes," she said through gritted teeth. "He got to Uoria and was stuck there because of the Covra. That's what allowed him to still be alive now and to come back to Earth."

"It might be possible in different ways, but the point is that they both happened and that they are both possible because of things that you didn't know existed. Sometimes you have to just trust rather than using your own perceptions and experiences to determine what is real and what is possible."

"I don't think that now is the time for you to start trying to be my father and teaching me about the world."

"I've always been your father, Aubrey," Frederick argued. "Just because I couldn't be with you every day doesn't mean that I didn't love you and it doesn't mean that I wasn't doing everything that I could. You can't just pretend that I never saw you or that I never did anything for you. I wish that things could have been different, but they couldn't be."

"Why not? You said that you were working as a part of trying to stop Ryan, but if you and Jonah could have supposedly been gone from the factory for years in your timeline and yet got back within a few minutes after I had last seen him, why were you gone for years when I was younger? Why haven't I seen you in years now?"

"I haven't been able to be with you recently because I knew the time was coming that you were going to be thrown into this and I couldn't interfere. I never wanted my daughter to have to face the danger and the fear that has been a part of my daily life since I became a part of this, but I knew that there was nothing that I could do to protect you. If I let myself get near you, I would try to stop it from happening, and that could cause cataclysmic results. So, I had to stay away from you. I couldn't let myself try to stand in the way and keep you out of it. Even if I thought that it would protect you, the ripples that it would cause could be devastating and, in the end, I would be causing you even more pain."

"What do you mean? How could you have known that I was a part of this? And it still doesn't explain why you were gone for so long when I was younger."

"Time is not finite. It can be manipulated. It can be changed. Though few know how, it is possible to move through it when given the right skills. But the progression of time is finite. No matter how much you try to manipulate time or how much you move through it, it will always be going ahead. There is flexibility in what will happen in time and how it can be shaped, but that is not always the case. In that forward progression there are moments, fixed moments that provide structure to existence. If those events are altered, everything could begin to break apart. You are one of those fixed moments. When you came into being there were two options for how time could move forward with you in it. How all of existence was impacted was determined by which path that you took. One meant near-certain disaster. One gave a chance for survival."

"How could I possibly make that much of a difference?" Aubrey asked. "I'm just one person."

"You're just one person, but you are a piece of something much bigger. How you work within that bigger picture is what makes you so critical. It's also what made it so that I couldn't be near you. You needed to fulfill your part, even if that meant that I had to allow you to be in danger, because if I stopped it, the entire Universe could fall. If you hadn't grown up when and how you did, if you didn't interact with the people that you did, if you didn't find Jonah when and how you did, then the work of many people would be lost and the deaths of even more would have been in vain."

"But I haven't done anything."

"But you have. And you will do so much more. That's what Jonah and I were trying to understand. We were trying to uncover the exact role that you play and why. But we couldn't. We still have to piece it together, but now that you know, we will be able to work on it together."

"How do you know that I'm supposed to do anything?"

"Your patient file," Jonah said.

"My file?"

"Yes. We found that in the abandoned medical facility. A facility that wasn't supposed to be there anymore and was only there because of the Izalux and the records."

"Yes. But it doesn't make any sense."

"Exactly. The dates on it don't make sense. The fact that

you went to the doctor three days in a row doesn't make sense. But the question that has bothered me the most is why that one page was missing and where it went."

"And you know why?" Aubrey asked, looking at Frederick.

He shook his head.

"No. But I once knew someone who did. And it has to do with the years that I spent away from you when you were younger."

"Tell me."

"I will, but now we need to leave. We can't stay in one place for too long. Ryan will be looking for us."

He turned and walked out of the room, leaving Aubrey with no choice but to go back into the bedroom and get her bags. Jonah walked in behind her and picked up his bags. She looked up at him.

"How could any of this be real? How could I have anything to do with this when I don't even know what's happening?"

"I don't know, Aubrey. I wish there was more that I could tell you."

"But there is. You could tell me what you've been doing all this time. You could tell me what caused that scar."

"I'll tell you everything. But Frederick is right. We need to keep moving. The poison in the arrows that we used against the Valdicians doesn't last forever. The paralyzing effect is only temporary. Escaping from the factory was never something that Ryan intended. As soon as he found out that we were there, he thought that he finally had his hands on the hybrids and breeders that he had lost, and on us. Getting Ilya back under his control is extremely important to him and knowing that Frederick was a part of the escape only made him angrier. He's going to be looking for us. We've reached a breaking point now. There's no turning back. No hesitation. Ryan has started to lose control and isn't as careful anymore. That means that we and all the others working against him are getting to him, but it also means that everyone in his path is in so much more danger. Until we can connect with the others and put all the pieces in place, we need to stay out of his grasp."

THEY RODE along in silence again, each vigilant, each focused on what was happening beyond the windows. They were looking for anything that might indicate that Ryan was tracing them. It was well into the afternoon before Aubrey realized that she didn't recognize the direction that they were going. She had thought that by this point it would look familiar and that she would be able to gauge how much farther it would be until they reached Nana's house, but when she examined the world outside of the window, she realized that nothing looked familiar.

"Where are we?" she asked, breaking the tense silence in the car. "How far are we from Nana's house?"

Frederick hesitated and glanced at Jonah, but he didn't say anything or even acknowledge the older man. Instead, he reached over and took Aubrey's hand, squeezing it as if he could recognize that she needed the comfort of his touch right then. Frederick glanced in the rearview mirror at her briefly before turning his attention back to the road in front of him.

"We aren't going back to Nana's house," he said.

Aubrey felt like the last of her grasp on her life was draining out of her. A burning started in her stomach as if a hot rock was settled there.

"What do you mean we're not going back to Nana's house?"

"It's too dangerous. There are still vulnerable women and hybrids there. She is their only hope at staying safe right now and if we were to go back there we could lure Ryan or the Valdicians straight to them. For now, we have to stay away from there. It will be much easier for us to avoid him than it would be for them to stay safe if he was to find them."

"Where are we going?"

"Ryan wants Ilya. I don't know why, but he is focused on her. We need to keep her safe."

"I thought that you said that this was about me," Aubrey said.

"You are a critical part of it," Frederick said. "You have responsibilities that you will need to fulfill. But for now, Ryan's concentration is on Ilya and getting his hands on her again. Above all the other women who were in the facility and beyond any of the hybrids that he has made, he wants her. So, we need to bring her to where he isn't going to be able to find her."

"Where is that?"

"Before Ryan was born."

11

"You wanted to talk to us?"

George looked up as Jem and Angela came into the infirmary. He noticed Angela glance at the bones that were still spread out on the table and then turn away, focusing her eyes on one of the empty tables instead. He realized that he likely should have covered the body before having them come in, but it hadn't occurred to him. He was accustomed to seeing bones this way, removed from the rest of the body that they had once supported, the last remaining vestige of the life that had existed for a time. No matter how long that person lived, the time that stretched between the moment of its birth and the last of its breaths never seemed long enough. It was so brief, just a momentary flash against the expanse of all of time and space that had and would exist. George honored the bones for that reason. They lasted so much longer than the skin that had touched and was touched, the eyes that saw, the tongue that spoke, the lips that brushed against those of loved ones. It was the bones that stayed long after all that identified the person as an individual with just a glance disappeared, all that was left to tell the story of who and what that person was and the life that they had led.

George was fascinated by all that the bones contained. When he was on Earth his laboratory would have been equipped with the tools and technology that would have been able to look further into the bones and delve into all that they could tell him. Those bones held everything that he needed to know who they had belonged to and possibly even what had happened to him. Here, though, he didn't have the comfort and reassurance of that technology. As he looked at the bones now he realized just how much he relied on all of that in everything that he did. When he investigated or researched. When he tried to understand something or explored more of what he had already found. In every aspect of his scientific work, the first thing that he did was figure out which machine or tool or computer program he could use to guide him. He had stopped relying as much on his instincts. Now that he was here on Penthos he had none of those tools. All he had was the few resources available to him in the ship infirmary and the knowledge and instincts that had driven him into the scientific field. It was a rediscovery and he found himself savoring the freedom. He wouldn't be able to see the bones as an experiment or something he could analyze. Instead, he was going to have to learn about them by exploring not what was left of the life, but the life itself.

"Yes. Thank you for coming," George said.

They seemed unfazed by having traveled across the planet so quickly and George realized it was because they were both accustomed to the concept of the portals that turned trips that should take hours or even days and turned them into mere seconds. It was something that they had both done countless times. It was what had brought them together.

"Rilex said that you were investigating a body," Jem said. "This is it?"

"Yes. He and Severine found it in the tunnel. They asked me to find out what I could about it and I think that I might have uncovered something telling. But I'm not sure."

"What is it?"

"First, could I see the bracelet that you're wearing?"

Jem looked at him quizzically.

"My bracelet?"

"Yes. When you first arrived back you were wearing a bracelet that you said Angela made for you before you made your way back to Earth and then to Uoria. Are you still wearing it?"

Jem glanced down at his arm and pushed his sleeve up to reveal the bracelet still attached around his wrist. It looked more worn than it had when he had first arrived, the plants that comprised it darkened and slightly frayed from being in place on his wrist through everything that Jem had gone through in the time since he got back home. The Denynso warrior held his arm out toward George, who took his wrist and examined the bracelet.

"And you made this?" he asked, looking up at Angela.

She nodded.

"Jem told me that he had never celebrated Christmas. When I first met Galadriel, I asked her what day it was on Earth and was able to figure out how far we were from the holidays, and I wanted to be able to celebrate it with Jem. I had told him about the traditions and I wanted to give him a gift. During the time that I was in the jungle with him, I had done some exploring and found the different kinds of plants with different colors of leaves. I thought that I could use them to make something for him, so I made a bracelet."

"What does my bracelet have to do with this body?" Jem asked.

George released Jem's arm and walked over to the other table where he had placed the dish holding the leaf. He held it out to Jem and Angela.

"Is this the leaf?" he asked.

Both looked into the dish and Angela looked up at him, nodding.

"I think so. I mean, that one is dried out, but it looks like the same type of leaf that I used."

"I found this on the body," George said. "I had never seen an actual one of them before. The truth is, I thought that it wasn't real."

"What do you mean?"

"When I was on Earth, Ivy and I were doing research about a document found many years ago. We found it when we were doing more extensive digging into the Denynso in preparation for the University exchange program with Uoria. We had gone off the original plans and found some of the lesser known stories and legends about the planet. That's how we found the document. It talked about a war that the Denynso were a part of but that had occurred off Uoria."

Jem shook his head.

"No," he said. "The Denynso haven't fought off the planet. We protect Uoria. It's our purpose. Uoria is the jewel of the galaxy, the most desirable of all destinations. It is the home of the most powerful creatures outside of Earth in the entire Universe. Our kind has stayed here and faced down the species who have tried to invade or who have wanted to earn the right to take over by defeating us. War happens on the battlefields of the compound, not outside of it."

"That was what we had heard about the warriors, too," George confirmed. "But this document detailed a war where the warriors left Uoria to aid another species. They were brought in to help fight during an uprising that tore apart an alliance and that resulted in the expulsion of an entire species from the planet where they had lived. It said that the planet was contained within the constellation Cassiopeia. There were a few details about the planet, including sketches of the plant life. One of the sketches looked like this leaf."

"What are you saying?" Angela asked.

"I think that we know where Jem was when he disappeared. And where this man was before he died."

RILEX LOOKED distracted and upset when George rushed up to him. He had already sent the man to get Jem and Angela from the compound, but now he needed to speak just to him. Jem and Angela came up behind him and Rilex looked surprised to see all of them approaching.

"Is everything alright?" he asked.

George tried to ignore the miserable look on Rilex's face as he gestured behind him.

"Can you come speak to us?"

Rilex nodded and George led them into one of the lounges in the ship, closing the door behind them so that no one else could hear what they were discussing. He knew that eventually, if they were right, the rest would have to know what he had uncovered. For now, though, he didn't want anyone else to overhear. They needed to keep the information close, protected until they figured out if George was right and what it could mean if he was.

Rilex, Jem, and Angela sat in the chairs positioned near the blocked window and George took the final chair. He leaned toward Rilex and withdrew the dish with the leaf from his pocket. Holding it out to Rilex, he waited for a reaction. The man stared at it for several long, silent seconds and then lifted his hand to run his fingers over the glass the covered the leaf.

"Do you recognize it?" George finally asked.

Rilex looked up at him and George saw the unusual pattern in his eyes, the shooting stars that marked him as something so different than the rest of them. There was something in those eyes, a distant look of nostalgia and memories, and a hint of something sad.

"I do," he said. "But I don't understand. How did you get this leaf? You shouldn't have been able to access it. No one should."

"Why?"

"This leaf comes from a species of tree that only exists on one planet in the Universe. I haven't seen it in..." he hesitated and let out a sigh, "a long time."

"This leaf is from the place where I was when Vyker and Galadriel found me," Jem said. "It's from where Angela and I stayed before we went back to Earth to go to Uoria."

Rilex shook his head.

"No," he said. "That's not possible."

"What do you mean it's not possible?" Jem asked.

"That planet is inaccessible. It has been since I lived in my stream. In your time, that is thousands of years ago."

"What do you mean it's inaccessible?" George asked.

"It was sealed long ago by my best friend, Malan. Mhavrych's grandfather."

"Mhavrych?" Jem asked, sounding startled. "Mhavrych is Vyker and Galadriel's son?"

"Yes," Rilex said. "She was carrying him when they sealed the wall."

George was unsure of what they were talking about, but he knew that it carried tremendous significance to them.

"What do you mean it was sealed?"

Rilex took the leaf from George's hand and stared down at it again.

"There was a war," he said. "Malan wanted to ensure that no one traveled to that planet again. He wanted it protected, but he also wanted to protect any who might be tempted to go there."

"Why?" George asked.

"The war divided two species. My kind is known as the Kintani. We are the creators of the stars and the protectors of the knowledge of the Universe. At the time we were also the guardians of another species, a species that we had saved from total destruction."

"The Travetori."

Rilex looked at George sharply.

"How do you know that?"

"I thought it was a legend," he said. "I didn't think that it was real."

"What?" Jem asked. "What are you talking about?"

"I told you about the document that I found that described the war that involved the Denynso. That is the war between the Kintani and the Travetori."

"Why was there a war?" Angela asked.

"The Kintani had been guardians over the Travetori for generations. They had tried to take over several species and were nearly successful until an uprising among some of them put the entire species at risk. My kind rescued them, but only with the understanding that they would live under our conditions. That included living on a planet that had previously been hidden from all others. We surrounded the planet with the constellation of Cassiopeia, ensuring that it was both protected and protector. On that planet, they would be inaccessible from the enemy races that wanted to destroy them, but they would also be controlled and prevented from seeking the power that they had been trying to gain through invasion and destruction. There were three brothers. The youngest, Jiri, had just been given the position of King, much to the anger of his brothers. His parents believed that their middle son was planning a rebellion against him, but it was actually the other son, their oldest child, who had been strategizing for some time, preparing for mutiny that would lead to war, determined to free himself and those who agreed to follow him from the control of the Kintani so that they could return to the pursuit of dominance in the Universe that he believed was the birthright of the species."

"Why were the Denynso brought in?" George asked.

"The Travetori had never concealed their desire to conquer the Denynso. Even then they were known as the most powerful warriors in all the Universe. With them under their power, there would be nothing that could stop them. The Kintani wanted to bring them in to fight in the war to show the ongoing dominance of the Denynso and to end the conflict as quickly as possible. Before the war began, Malan commanded that Cassiopeia be evacuated. All who were not going to fight were to be taken from the planet and brought to another planet where they would be completely sealed off so that they could not be accessed throughout the rest of their existence. They were free to live out their lives there. The only ones who were not brought to that planet immediately were Jiri, his partner Layla, and a few close members of their group. They were brought to Uoria for protection. After the war, Malan returned to Uoria with the Denynso and then sealed off the way between Uoria and Cassiopeia, completing the total seal so that no one would ever find that planet again."

"I've never heard of the Kintani," George said. "Or the Travetori."

"Neither have I," Angela said.

"You wouldn't," Rilex said. "We're no longer known."

"I remember Galadriel saying that," Jem said. "When she and Vyker found me, she pointed out that we came from the same time, but that was a different time than Vyker. She told him that we didn't know about his kind or what they did."

"That's true," Rilex said.

"Then why is it a problem that the planet wasn't actually sealed? To us, the war was thousands of years ago. It must have been successful."

"No," Rilex said. "It wasn't. Not fully."

"What do you mean?"

"During the war, the majority of those who had followed the brother and believed in his cause were killed. But the brother and several of his closest followers managed to escape into the streams. They had to go into hiding and over time seemed to fade, but then they re-emerged. Weaker, but still present. By then the brother had died, but his followers continued to honor him."

"How?" Angela asked.

"The brother that started the war was named Valdin."

Jem's jaw tightened, and George saw his orange eyes flash angrily.

"The Valdicians."

12

TO BE CONTINUED...

Mhavrych didn't want to go back into the prison. He had thought that he would only have to experience the horrific place once, but following Kendra had brought him back here, forcing him back into the grotesque hallways and grungy cells that still carried the feeling of despair and torture that he could only imagine seeped into the stone when it held the countless prisoners. He stayed in the darkest shadows even when he wanted to move toward the light when the Denynso opened the trapdoor that led down into the dungeon. Even more than he hadn't wanted to come back to the prison he hadn't wanted to go down into the dungeon beneath the already gruesome floors of the building. The upper floors of the building were already heavy and filled with signs of the brutality that had happened there. Opening the trapdoor and dropping down into the dark, damp section of the building felt like he was putting himself in the place of the inmates.

The feeling of being in the dungeon crawled across his skin and Mhavrych felt the uncomfortable feeling rolling down his spine. He had known that the Denynso were coming and it was all that he could do to stand there and wait rather than getting out of the building. When he finally heard the footsteps of the men above him he was too relieved to no longer be completely alone in the eerie building to even consider that it might not be the warriors and instead could be the Valdicians or even the Covra returning to the building that was a monument of victory to them rather than a sign of torment. The thought only occurred to him when the door opened overhead, and he heard the voices coming down toward him. He pushed back against one of the corners and watched the dusty light come down from the ceiling, surrounding the group of warriors. He watched as they came into the basement, looking around just as he had done when he first came inside.

They had been exploring the cold, musty hallways for nearly an hour, Mhavrych creeping carefully behind them so that his footsteps were concealed by theirs and he could watch what they were doing without being detected, when Ty discovered a door. It was sitting on what seemed to be an otherwise blank wall. This door didn't look as though it led into one of the cells and the handle didn't shift under his hand when he tried to open it. Finally, he took a step back and directed a forceful kick into the center of the door. The aged wood splintered beneath his foot and Ty immediately pushed through the broken pieces to enter the small room. Mhavrych couldn't see into the room from his vantage point, but he eased as close as he could to hear what they were saying.

"Hey, Pyra," Ty yelled from inside the room.

Pyra rushed past Mhavrych without noticing him and entered the room. Mhavrych saw the shine of a light within the room.

"What did you find?"

"What do you know about this prison?" Ty asked.

"Not much. I didn't even know it was here until the Klimnu attacked. I'm guessing that they built it so long ago that no one remembers it."

"I don't think they built it at all."

"What do you mean?"

"Look at this."

"Holy shit."

"I know."

Listening to the conversation was frustrating. Mhavrych wanted to know what they were looking at, what was interesting them so much. All he could do was listen and take in as much information as he could until they left so he could explore the room for himself. Ero walked into the room and Mhavrych moved slightly closer, risking rushing past the open door and into the deeper darkness toward the end of the hallway. He trusted that the men were distracted enough that they wouldn't notice the flash of his movement across the doorway. From the position he could see part of the room through the door and noticed that it was an office with a desk on one wall and rows of bookshelves along the other.

"What's going on?" Ero asked.

"This prison wasn't built by the Klimnu," Pyra said.

"What do you mean?"

"Ty just found all of these books and papers. It looks like the Klimnu were just about as gracious with this prison as they were with the realm under the compound. Apparently, this prison has been here for hundreds of years, which means that it was built before the Denynso were living on the compound."

"How could we not know that?"

"I don't know. Creia said that our kind has never made

contact with other species except in battle. If it was there when the Denynso settled the compound, they either didn't notice it, or the species that built it was already gone by the time they came."

"How is that even possible?" Ero asked.

"I don't know."

"Look at this."

Mhavrych could see Pyra and noticed that he was holding a small book in his hands. His eyes were scanning across the pages as he seemed to be taking in as much as he could from it.

"This says that the species that built this prison built it during a war with another species that they had been in conflict with for years. They used this prison to hold people who they captured during battle, but the other species found out and infiltrated the prison, freeing all of the captives and killing many of the Covra."

"The Covra?"

Mhavrych recognized the name of the species both from what the group had told him about Nyx 23 and from the stories that his parents had told him about Uoria.

"That's what it says. I've never heard of that species before."

"What happened after that battle?"

"This says that the Covra knew they weren't strong enough to fight off the rest of what they call the Light Ones, so they locked them."

"Locked them?" Ty asked.

"It says that the Covra can lock an entire area in place. It's like the whole place is frozen in time. They at once exist and don't. Time passes around them, but it doesn't impact them. They locked the entire kingdom of the Light Ones in that moment and never made any plans to release them."

Pyra paused for a moment and in an instant Mhavrych had the same thought that Pyra expressed.

"What if they're still there?"

Mhavrych realized that they were talking about the Nyx 23 crew and the settlement that they had created. He knew that he had heard them talking about the crew and its appearance on Uoria, but he had been so focused on what he had come to the planet to do that he hadn't thought much of it. He had done little to really learn about them or what their presence meant. Now he felt as though he was learning more, like he was standing alongside the Denynso as they discovered this new element of their beloved planet.

"What do you mean?" Ero asked.

"There's a map right here that shows where everything was when this all happened," Pyra said, indicating something on the page in front of him. "What if the kingdom is still there and the Light Ones are still stuck there, just like they have been since the Covra locked them?"

"Pyra?"

Lynx had come to the door and was standing just a few feet from Mhavrych. Mhavrych pressed his body harder into the corner, holding his breath so that he wouldn't be detected. He didn't know what would happen if the warriors discovered that he was there with them. In their timeline, none of them had encountered or even heard of Mhavrych. Though he wouldn't say that he had any real connection with any of the men in that room now, having spent little or no time with them personally, he knew who each of them were and a few details about them. If they were to see him, however, they would know nothing about him and would have no reason to believe him when he told them who he was or where he came from. He didn't fear the men or the fight that might start if that happened. Instead, he feared how it might affect all that had already happened and all that still needed to happen if they were to clash too soon.

"What is it, Lynx?" Pyra asked.

"There really isn't much down here. A bunch of cells. A couple of old chains."

"Tell the men to find a way to get back up out of the trapdoor and gather up outside. Our little adventure here is taking a detour."

That was the first indication to Mhavrych that there were more of the warriors in the prison. He hoped that he had followed the right group and was going to find what he needed to.

"Where are we going?"

"Back in time, it looks like."

The words sank into Mhavrych and somehow, he knew that was the indication that he was waiting for. He had done what he was supposed to do and now he only needed to keep going. He hadn't seen Kendra since getting to the prison, but he had learned to sense her presence, to know what she had intended for him to do. He still didn't understand it. He still didn't know how she could know what she did or why she was sending him on this quest, but his feelings for her were getting stronger and now he felt like it was another element of his mission, another part of what was going to drive him. No longer was he doing this just because it was what his family expected of him. No longer was this just something that he was born to do. Now he was doing this for her and the life that they had both begun and had waiting for them.

The men streamed out of the room and Mhavrych waited until they were back up through the trapdoor and the door was in place before he used the orb of light from his bag to illuminate the space around him. The light cutting through the darkness created a protective halo and he felt warmed and reassured by the glow. Holding the orb in his hand reminded him again of the day that he had gone down into the lair of the Order to rescue Malcolm and used the orb to trigger the lights in the corridor. He could still feel the orb hit his ankle when it landed on the platform that he had climbed onto. He hadn't been able to understand it, to figure out how it had gotten out of the corridor and back up with him. Now he knew. It had been Kendra. She had been with him even then.

Surrounded by light that Mhavrych now associated with Kendra, he walked into the room that the Denynso men had just left. Just as he had assumed, it was an office. There were papers strewn across the desk and Mhavrych glanced over some of them, trying to find what the warriors had been discussing. He didn't notice a map or the book that Pyra had been holding and he realized that they must have taken it with them. The longer that he looked at the papers, the stronger a realization became. This prison had been overrun with Klimnu, and yet the papers were about the Valdicians and the Covra. They were in far better condition that Mhavrych would have expected them to be after the many years that had passed since either species had been in this prison and he found it strange that the Klimnu had left them where they were.

Mhavrych gathered the papers and slipped them into the satchel that he had brought with him. He didn't think that he was going to find out anything more here in the prison. He would have to take his time going through the papers, and possibly share them with the others, to find out what they meant.

He paused to listen at the trapdoor for a few seconds to make sure that he didn't hear any of the Denynso. When only silence greeted him, he extinguished his light orb and tucked it away before climbing up and out of the dungeon. He was relieved when he finally got out of the charred remains of the prison and out into the fresher air. Around him the forest was silent. He couldn't hear any of the warriors or the women. At this point, they had returned to their village and were preparing for the next day, the momentous day when they would leave the compound for the first time. Of them, only one of the warriors had been beyond the large walls that surrounded the compound. Only Ero had ever left, and then it was aboard a ship that brought him to Earth so that he could make amends with his mate after hurting her with a cruel and thoughtless comment he had never intended for her to hear and had said only with the hopes of impressing the other men.

Mhavrych stood several yards away from the prison and waited. He expected Kendra to come as she always did, to reassure him, to guide him, to give him another of the riddles that were both infuriating and leading. After several long minutes, though, she hadn't gotten there. He was still alone and soon he resigned himself to the fact that he didn't come here just to go through the prison again. Instead, there was something more that he needed to do. He suspected that he knew exactly what it was.

The weather was mild and the moon high and bright, telling Mhavrych it would be a good night to camp out rather than trying to find shelter. Not wanting to stay so close to the prison, he went deeper into the woods and found a thick knot of trees that were close enough to create a raised network of roots perfect for creating into a bed. Mhavrych settled onto the moss that stretched across the roots and pulled the papers out of his satchel again. Enough light filtered through the leaves of the trees overhead to allow him to read the papers and he went over them again. Though some were written in what looked like a shorthand code that he didn't understand, some were written clearly, and he read through them several times. It seemed that many of the notes that were written had been recorded at different times. It was almost like a scattered, unorganized journal, as though someone had come into this office and jotted down what he was thinking or had experienced without any real consideration of how it was recorded or if he would be able to decipher it later.

Mhavrych noticed something and read back through the papers again. It was a quick comment, something that seemed almost like an afterthought rather than something that held any importance, but it struck him hard. Amid several hastily written comments in the coded language that he didn't yet understand, Mhavrych saw a mention that while the Mikana had been maintaining a strong link with the settlement of Light Ones since their arrival, recent attempts to visit had been unsuccessful because the settlement seemed to have disappeared. He thought about what Aegeus and Casimir had told him, confirming that the Irisa had not only cloaked Aegeus during the battle to give him protection as he left, but had also been responsible for hiding the settlement. They had created a cloaking mechanism over the entrance to the settlement so that someone couldn't find them.

This thought rolled through his head several times. The settlement had been cloaked, hidden so that it couldn't be found. But in doing that it had also been kept from those who had been cooperating with them for years. They couldn't find them, which meant that there was a reason to protect them. Someone had discovered that they were locked and didn't know how to help them and so they protected them, hoping that eventually they could find a way to release them. They had no way of knowing that the Denynso would discover the presence of the settlement and go to look for it, guided by a map. It was that map that made a difference. When the Mikana tried to find the settlement, they traveled by memory and simply looked for it. They found it by sight. When they were unable to see it, they believed that it was somehow gone, which allowed the cloaking effect to stay effective. For the Denynso, though, it was different. They had a map. They knew exactly where the settlement was supposed to be and because of that and the fact that they had never seen the settlement, they had no reason to think that they wouldn't see it. That dissolved the concealment.

This meant that when the next day came, Mhavrych would be able to go to the settlement with them and witness the first time that they saw it. He only had to find a way to follow them without being detected. He knew that the warriors would be more vigilant during their first experience outside of the compound. No matter how courageous they were, this was unknown to them. They didn't know what they were going to see or what they were going to encounter on this first venture beyond the wall. This would intensify their defensiveness and make them more aware of what was going on around them. They would be quick to attack. Mhavrych would need to utilize every bit of his skill and subtlety to trace their movements without revealing that he was there.

He thought about this, trying to convince himself that it was something he could do, but Mhavrych was accustomed to the rest of the planet by now. He knew that the center stretch was often harsh with open sections that would provide no protection or diversion. If he was following the

Denynso, he would be fully visible with no place to disappear to. That meant that he didn't have the option of simply following along behind them as he had before or hiding nearby as he had in the prison. He would have to do something else, something that would allow him to be there to see whatever it was that Kendra intended for him to witness while also making sure that he was kept safely secured away from them. They couldn't be distracted. They couldn't be stopped. If they noticed him, Mhavrych knew they would likely strike first, but even if that was not their first instinct, what would be was them taking him and bringing him to Creia. Though facing the Denynso King also didn't frighten Mhavrych because he knew that he would be able to explain himself and his connections in a way that would protect him, the time that the warriors would waste bringing him there could mean that they didn't return to their quest. Even if they did, they might not find the settlement in time to rescue those who were trapped within.

Mhavrych soon realized that there would be no way for him to follow the Denynso warriors. If he was going to be there to witness their arrival and to see what they did, he was going to have to be there first. That meant he was going to have to either walk or find another way there. He didn't know if there were any tunnels that led to the settlement, but he highly doubted it. The tunnels and portals were ancient, established long before the settlement was built from the wreckage of the StarCity. The chances that they would build it near the network were slim. Besides, even if there was a connection near the settlement, Mhavrych was still unfamiliar with the surroundings. He might get himself confused or lost, and there were too many dangers and not enough time to face them.

Remembering the last time that he had seen Kendra,

Mhavrych stood and made his way through the forest until he reached the orchard. Here he pulled aside the large pieces of moss that covered the entry points to the mirror-image realm beneath. He slipped down into one of them and soon found himself in the cavern where he had witnessed the battle with the Klimnu and Jem's disappearance. He could hear voices and realized that one of the Denynso was in the realm with Loralia. This must have been early in her relationship with Bannack.

Using the volume of the voices as his guide, Mhavrych moved carefully through the space, avoiding making noise or getting close enough to them that they would know that he was there. Soon he made it through the main section and was in the tunnels that Kendra had shown him. He walked through them and out into the beautiful grounds of the Eteri village. As soon as he saw the hills with the small houses built into them, Mhavrych started to feel unsure of himself. He didn't know if this was the right thing to do, but he also felt as though this was where Kendra had guided him. She had brought him to her house, a house she claimed that they shared even though none of the Eteri had recognized him, so that he could have shelter for the night even though she knew that he had camped out many times before. He felt like she did that purposely, to show him the way and have a reason to introduce him to the man he was looking for now.

He had been walking through the still, quiet village for several minutes before he noticed any sign of anyone being awake. A woman came out of one of the buildings and looked at him. Though she would have had no reason to think that he would be standing there, she hadn't seemed startled. Instead, she seemed almost amused and fascinated by the new stranger standing in front of her. Mhavrych searched his mind for her name, knowing that he had seen her briefly during his last time in the village, but couldn't bring it to his tongue.

"Mhavrych," the woman said, startling him.

"Yes," he said, not knowing how else to respond.

She tilted her head at him and it suddenly occurred to him that in this timeline, he had already been here before. They had seen him, and a few had met him. He wasn't the total stranger that he thought himself to be. He took a step toward the young woman and tried to give what he hoped was a reassuring smile.

"Why are you back here? You shouldn't be here yet."

"Yet?"

"Kendra isn't here."

"I wasn't looking for her," he said, though in his heart he was. "I need to speak to Amoran."

"Amoran? What would you need with him?"

Her responses were odd and Mhavrych found himself feeling as though there was something he was missing.

"I just need to speak to him. I need to ask him to do a favor for me."

"I'm sure that he'll be happy to do anything that he can for you."

The woman disappeared and Mhavrych continued to try to remember her name. He was still thinking about it when he heard footsteps coming toward him and looked up to see Amoran. The large Eteri man was looking at him as quizzically as the woman had. He paused for a moment and then took a step toward Mhavrych.

"What are you doing here?" he asked.

"I need your help."

"Where is my sister?"

"Excuse me?"

"I haven't seen Kendra since the last time that you arrived."

Mhavrych's stomach sank.

"I don't know," he said. "I haven't seen her in some time, either. But I need your help. If you help me, we might be able to find her."

Amoran thought about this for a few seconds and then gave a barely perceptible nod.

"What do you need?"

"I need you to fly me," Mhavrych said.

"Excuse me?"

"Just like you did the first night that I met you. I need you to fly me. I need to get somewhere on the planet as fast as possible, and you are the fastest creature that I know. Will you please help me?"

"Where do you need to go?" Amoran asked.

Mhavrych weighed his explanation carefully. He wanted him to understand the importance of him getting there, but at the same time, he also needed to balance what he told him with the protection of what needed to happen in the order in which it needed to happen.

"I'm not completely sure," Mhavrych answered honestly. "I know that it is beyond the Denynso compound. It's a settlement. It's been there for many years, but no one has been near it in quite some time. I need to find it. It is extremely important."

Mhavrych knew that he would be able to see the settlement from the sky, making the flight with Amoran the perfect way to get to it as fast as possible. If he were approaching it walking the way the Mikana did, there was a strong chance that he wouldn't be able to see it because he didn't know the exact position where it was, and it was possible that he would be taken in by the cloaking performed by the Irisa. From the air, however, he wasn't controlled by that. The Irisa had hidden only the front gate of the settlement so that it couldn't be seen. That meant that when he was high above it, he was still able to see the buildings and the roads. When it came into view, Mhavrych felt a rush of excitement. He stared at it, not moving his eyes away from it, until he saw the front gate come into view.

It seemed to shimmer slightly as it appeared, as if it were unsure of its own existence after being hidden for so long. Amoran landed just outside of the gate and released the buckle that held the other man to his chest. Mhavrych thanked him and promised to let him know if he heard from Kendra, seeming to ease the Eteri man's suspicion and discomfort toward Mhavrych. As soon as Amoran had risen back into the sky to complete the brief flight back to his home village, Mhavrych turned to the arch that led into the settlement. What had once been a beautiful stone wall and arch was now weathered and crumbling, the arch covered in thick ivy. It looked as though no one had gone near it in decades, which Mhavrych knew in this timeline was exactly the case.

It felt strange to walk through the arch and into the village. He almost felt as though he were breaching their privacy, seeing things that he wasn't meant to see. And yet he could also feel that this was exactly where he was supposed to be. Using the moon to guide his way, he began to walk along the road that ran down the middle of the village. It had been painstakingly paved with stones taken from the nearby river and polished smooth to fit together along the path. All around him the settlement was utterly silent. The stillness was unnerving and when he encountered the first of the locked people, it sent a chill through him.

Somehow this wasn't what he expected when he went into the settlement. Though he had heard a description of what it was like there, he hadn't really envisioned what it must have been like to see these people caught in an instant, trapped in the middle of the breath that they were breathing. Nearly everything that they were doing was so completely mundane. Washing laundry. Shopping in the tiny store. Stopping to talk in the middle of the road. Stepping into the bakery. Somehow the fact that it was just another day made it even more disquieting. With something as cataclysmic as the Covra imprisoning an entire settlement for the purpose of using them as human incubators for their babies, Mhavrych would have envisioned a more chaotic sight. He would have wanted to feel as though they at least had a chance to fight.

He walked down the middle of the street, looking at each of the houses. Though built very similarly, they were also each unique. Each had touches and details that differentiated them from the rest, allowing Mhavrych to imagine the thought and energy that went into crafting these homes by those who had suffered and survived, and were forcing themselves to drive on, to push forward in the new life that had been cast onto them.

One house caught Mhavrych's eye and he stopped to look at it. There was something about it that was slightly different from the rest, though he couldn't quite place it. He turned and looked at each of the other houses that were close to it. This house was in the furthest back corner of the village, tucked slightly apart from the one beside it, but that seemed to be by design, allowing for a garden positioned in between the two houses that had long since died and been reclaimed by the wild plants. He could still see signs of what had been the rows of vegetables and tools embedded in the ground. He looked at the house again and realized what it was about the house that was different from the rest. It was smaller, almost as though it had been made as a guest house or in preparation for a young couple moving into it as their first home.

Mhavrych walked toward the house, the prickling feeling on the back of his neck telling him that his subconscious was just waiting for something to happen. His body was on alert, but even as he walked up to the door, nothing changed around him. He touched the door handle and it moved. The door opened far more easily than he would have anticipated. After all the years that had passed, he would have expected that there would have been resistance due to the door or the handle warping or being changed by the weather. Instead, the door opened easily, and he was able to step through into the house.

The house was welcoming if somewhat sparse. The door opened directly into a living room which held two sofas, a chair, and a table. The chair and table looked as though they had been salvaged directly from the crash rather than being built with the materials that could be taken from the wreckage. He ran his fingers along the back of one of the chairs and then rested his hand on the metal that made up the structure of one of the couches. Finally, he returned to his exploration.

The other houses looked as though they were at least two stories each. This house, however, was only one story. The ceilings were very high, accounting for the fact that the house looked only slightly smaller from the outside but was actually considerably smaller, if more open, on the inside. Ahead of him, he saw a door that he assumed led into the bedroom. He approached it cautiously, not sure of what he might find inside. He pushed the door open slowly by flattening his palm in the center of the door and gradually pressing it out of the way so that he could take in a small amount of the space at a time.

When the door was open, revealing the bedroom in front of him, Mhavrych noticed that there was someone in the bed. It was a sad image, a person resting, not knowing that their moments had been impossibly stretched but were also gravely limited. He felt drawn to the side of the bed, wanting to see the person's face. He knew from the description of what happened in the settlement after the Denynso arrived that not everyone survived. If this person was one of those who didn't live, he wanted to ensure that at least someone saw them alive one last time.

Mhavrych could see that the figure was a woman when he was still a few steps away. Her thick hair pooled around her head and spilled over the side of the bed, and a curvy body was tucked under a light blanket. Her hands were clasped over her chest. As he got closer, Mhavrych reached into the bag at his hip and withdrew one of the light orbs. He turned it on, filling the space with the soft glow, but nearly felt it slip from his fingertips when he turned his eyes back to the figure on the bed.

It was Kendra, her hands cradling the starstone nestled between her breasts.